VULTURE GOLD

Garet Havelock was Vulture City's marshal when outlaw Barnabas Donovan sent his men to rob $100,000 in bullion from the Vulture Mine headquarters. Whilst chasing the thieves across the Mojave Desert, Jicarilla Apaches forced Havelock and Donovan's bunch together in a cave on Eagle Eye Mountain. Then there was Laura Donovan, the outlaw leader's half-sister . . . Now Havelock must survive the Apache 'run of death', and face Donovan's gunslingers to get the gold and the girl.

CHUCK TYRELL

VULTURE GOLD

Complete and Unabridged

LINFORD
Leicester

First published in Great Britain in 2005 by
Robert Hale Limited
London

First Linford Edition
published 2006
by arrangement with
Robert Hale Limited
London

British Library CIP Data

Tyrell, Chuck
    Vulture gold.—Large print ed.—
Linford western library
    1. Western stories
    2. Large type books
    I. Title
    823.9′2 [F]

    ISBN 1–84617–358–2

Published by
F. A. Thorpe (Publishing)
Anstey, Leicestershire

Set by Words & Graphics Ltd.
Anstey, Leicestershire
Printed and bound in Great Britain by
T. J. International Ltd., Padstow, Cornwall

This book is printed on acid-free paper

1

The stench of death clung to the dry earth of Vulture City, a patch of hell on the Mojave Desert. The town's burgeoning jumble of dugouts, tarpaper shacks, and batten-on-plank houses fanned out from a plaza bordered by Garth's Mercantile and Vulture Mine headquarters, the Carrion saloon, the Vulture Hotel, and the marshal's office and jail. One street from the plaza ended at the Vulture Mine.

Gold sweetened the smell of death; pretty, plentiful gold from the Vulture Mine — richest in Arizona, maybe richest in the West.

The stamp-mill crushed the ore sweated from the mother lode and separated the gold from the quartz. Men with greed etched on their faces melted down the gold and poured it into forms for ingots an inch thick, three inches wide, and ten long. Each weighed about twenty-two ounces at fineness of just over 900.

Six boxes of twenty bars each stood stacked against the sides of the bullion-room pit at Vulture Mine headquarters. The iron grate that secured the pit leaned against the far wall, open for inventory. Ralph Judd carefully laid another ingot in a new box. Superintendent Harry Chambers sat in the back room at a table made of dynamite-crates and jotted entries in the ledger.

The instant an explosion rocked the face of the mine, half a mile away, three men barged into the bullion room with six-guns in their hands and bandannas covering their faces.

'Don't move!'

The order came from a tall white man with commanding ice-blue eyes beneath the rim of his dirty felt hat. The other two were Mexicans.

Judd's hands shot up and he froze, but Harry Chambers stepped from the back room and slammed the iron grate down on the bullion pit. Judd leaped for the padlock. His shaking fingers fumbled to fit it through the hasp.

'Gringo *hijo de puta!*' Two pistols spat flame almost as one. One bullet threw Judd across the iron grate in a sprawl. The padlock slipped from his dying fingers to splat in the blood on the pit's dirt floor.

The other bullet drilled Chambers' left shirt-pocket, punctured his heart, and slammed him wide-armed against the back wall. His dying spasms tipped him over to lie face down in his own gore. The bullion room filled with the coppery scent of ripped and bloody flesh and the offal odor of bowels voided in death.

The big man holstered his gun.

'Let's get that gold out of here,' he said sharply. The Mexicans ignored his unspoken disapproval of the shootings.

The trio quickly hauled the bullion from the pit and loaded it onto two pack-mules tethered outside. Four boxes went in canvas pouches strapped to the pack saddles. They lashed the remaining two bullion boxes to the forks.

'Move!' shouted the leader. The Mexicans roweled their horses and lunged away, jerking the gold-laden mules after them. The bandit leader rushed back into the bullion room for the ingots on Judd's desk.

★ ★ ★

The leader ran from the bullion room, threw a pair of saddle-bags across the skirt of his rig, and leaped into the saddle.

'Halt!' Marshal Garet Havelock roared. He'd hustled back from investigating the mine explosion but was still 200 yards away. He went down on one knee and jacked a shell into his Winchester.

The outlaw reined his horse around. He stared at Havelock, unafraid, then tilted back his head and laughed. The sound echoed from the stone walls of the buildings around the plaza. Havelock had heard that mocking laugh before, during darker times, and it brought unpleasant memories. The bandit lunged his horse toward the mountain trail out of town.

Havelock squeezed off a shot.

The horse reared wildly, almost going over. The big rider clung for a moment, then dropped off, arms and legs flailing. He landed head first, bounced, and lay face down. The startled mount raced for the trail, saddlebags jouncing.

Havelock levered a new cartridge into the chamber and waited, rifle to cheek. The downed outlaw lay still. Slowly the marshal stood, rifle held ready. By the time he reached the prone man, citizens of Vulture City began to appear in the plaza.

'Know who it is, Marshal?' Solomon Garth stood on the steps of his store.

'Yeah. It's Barnabas Donovan.'

Havelock knelt by the fallen man. Blood spread from under his right shoulder, mixing with the dust. The marshal put the muzzle of his rifle to the base of Donovan's head, then laid a finger to the artery in his neck — strong, steady pulse.

'Pappy!'

At Havelock's shout, jailer Pappy Holmes stuck his head out the door of the marshal's office.

'Get that 10-gauge Greener and get out here.'

A moment later, the old man stood by Havelock. He peered at the unconscious outlaw. Both hammers of the wicked sawed-off double-barreled shotgun were cocked.

'Hey!' A cry came from the bullion room. 'Judd and the super are dead!'

For an instant, Havelock saw a blackened body swinging from the ironwood hanging-tree and the death smell cloyed in his nostrils. He'd tried to stop the last lynching — a young drifter — but either the mob had been too much, or Havelock had not been enough. The boy hung there for three days while Havelock nursed his pride in the jail and the miners laughed at the half-breed marshal who couldn't stand up to their mobs.

Unless Havelock moved fast, Donovan too would swing from the hanging-tree. Havelock's tongue licked over thin, dry lips, but didn't leave much moisture behind. He scanned the crowd for some-one he could trust. Tom Morgan, huge and black, stood near Garth's store. He owed Havelock for Santa Fe.

'Tom Morgan,' Havelock called.

Morgan moved through the crowd, his face impassive.

'Help Pappy get this body into the jailhouse, if you would.'

Morgan nodded. He shifted his Ballard .50 so it hung beneath his left armpit, muzzle down. Havelock took the Greener shotgun from Pappy, who moved to grab the outlaw's knees. Morgan motioned him away and picked up the unconscious body in his great arms as if it were a child, and carried Donovan into the jailhouse.

'Wil Jacks.'

'Right here, Marshal.'

'We're going to need nine good horses, Wilford. Make one of them my grulla. And saddle Tom Morgan's mule, if you please.'

Jacks hurried off and Havelock turned to the angry crowd. He took a deep breath, and scowled to hide his unease.

'OK. I want those killers worse than you do. We've got one, and we'll get the others. I want eight men to go with me and Tom Morgan.'

Almost everyone clamored to go, but a few hung back, not willing to ride out with a 'breed and a black. God. It seemed like every time he proved himself, he had to turn around and do it all over again. Havelock raised his hand, and the crowd quieted.

'Benson, Dailey, Decker, Smythe, Foggarty, Swenson, Carson, Mills. Hold up your right hands. Do you swear to uphold the law? OK, you're deputies. Meet me in front of the jail in five minutes. We'll probably be gone for a couple of days. Be ready.'

The men broke and ran to prepare.

'What's this about a dead man?'

Havelock didn't answer. He just started for the jail across the plaza. Though his left knee was stiff, his pace was swift. Doc Withers had to trot to keep up.

'What's your hurry? The jail isn't afire, and that man's dead, isn't he?'

'No.'

Doc Withers stuttered, but didn't stop. Havelock slammed the door after them as they entered the marshal's office. Pappy held the Greener dead center on Havelock's chest, and Morgan stood with his Ballard .50 rifle halfway to his shoulder.

'Most folks knock afore they come a-bustin' in,' Pappy said. He released the hammers on the shotgun and leaned it against Havelock's scarred wooden desk.

'Where's Donovan?' Havelock asked.

Pappy waved a hand toward the cells in the rear.

'Still out. First cell.'

'Come on, Doc.'

Donovan stirred as Havelock and Doc Withers entered the cell. The doctor felt his pulse and nodded.

'No problem with this man,' he said. 'Heartbeat like a horse's.' The doc continued his examination. 'Got a fair-sized knot on his head. But he's just unconscious. Now, let's have a look at that wound.'

Havelock's bullet had ripped a deep gash beneath Donovan's right arm. It had bled a lot, but wasn't life-threatening. Doc Withers stitched the wound and dressed it. As he straightened up, Donovan mumbled.

'Whass goin' on?'

The doctor cast a caustic look in Donovan's direction.

'Let me see. You're dead, and I'm Saint Peter. God and I have been discussing whether to send you to Hell now or put it off a while so the Devil can get some rest.' Doc snapped his black bag closed. 'Havelock, let me out of here.'

Havelock opened the cell door. Donovan's eyes followed the doctor out.

'Donovan.'

The outlaw turned his gaze on the marshal.

'Two men are dead in the bullion room across the way. I'm gonna see you swing for that.'

Donovan squeezed his eyes shut for a moment before replying.

'I've killed no one,' he said. He spoke slowly and carefully, as if talking made his head hurt.

'The hell you say.'

'Look at my gun. I've not fired it.'

'Pappy. Bring me Donovan's rig.'

The Greener appeared first, hammers cocked, followed by Pappy's relief-map face. He held out Donovan's fancy tooled-leather rig. Havelock pulled the bone-handled Smith & Wesson from the holster. He broke the gun open. The cylinder held five live bullets. The hammer had rested on an empty chamber.

Some of the sarcastic edge returned to Donovan's voice.

11

'Well, boy. Tell me. How did I kill anyone without firing my gun?' he said.

'Don't push it, Donovan. When I get through with you, you'll wish you were up for murder.' Havelock's ears burned at Donovan's calling him 'boy' but he wheeled on his good leg and strode back into the office.

Tom Morgan waited, ready to ride. Sounds outside said the posse was restless. Havelock tucked a trap-door Springfield rifle under his arm and picked up a box of .45–70 cartridges.

He stepped out of the jail with Morgan a half-pace behind. He stuffed the Springfield into the saddle scabbard and the shells into his off-side saddle-bag. Then he mounted his slate-gray grulla mustang from that same off-side. With a game knee, he couldn't mount a horse in the usual way.

'Listen up,' Havelock shouted. 'Two good men died today. And the mine's out a sight of gold. Now those thieves have a fifteen-minute start on us, but we can catch them. Morgan, lead out.'

The posse moved into the unforgiving desert which surrounded Vulture City. Morgan tracked as well as any Apache. And the outlaws, with their two mules, had left a trail even a tenderfoot could follow. The hoofprints led south toward the juncture of the Hassayampa and Gila rivers.

— The posse rode under the brassy sky for two hours before Havelock called a halt to rest and water the horses. The men sipped sparingly from their canteens and swabbed the horses' mouths with wet bandannas. The posse was silent, waiting for Havelock to say something. He sensed their trust, and vowed not to let them down. Wasn't often a Cherokee half-breed got respect.

'Where d'ya think they're headed, Tom?'

The black man shrugged. He hunkered down, picked up a dry mesquite twig, and sketched a rough map.

'This here's the Hassayampa. If they keep on going like this, they'll hit the big bend of the Gila, right here.'

13

Morgan's twig struck a rough S for the Gila River, and drew the crooked line of the Hassayampa joining it at the top left-hand curve.

'Them rowdies could be headed for Dixie, but I can't see that town giving them much of a welcome. They could be going to Surprise Well, east and south of Woolsey Butte. And they could strike out for the Bosque Wood camp over across the Hassayampa. Now, that's what I figure they'll do, cross that ford just above the old Richards place.' Morgan paused and chewed on the twig. 'Havelock, I don't like the way them Mexes shuffled they trail here. They up to no good. Count on it.'

Havelock nodded. 'You're probably right. We'd better cover our bets. You know where Surprise Well is. Take four men, I'll take the rest. I'll cover Richards Crossing. You hit Surprise. Either way, we're bound to get them. But keep your eyes peeled.'

'I'll do it.'

The posse mounted up.

14

'Benson. Decker. Mills. Swenson. You four go with Morgan to Surprise Well. Benson, you're in charge. If they go that way, you get 'em.' Havelock made it look like the white man was the leader. Morgan understood.

'Rest of you ride with me. Let's cut those killers off at Richards Crossing. Move out!'

*   *   *

Havelock and his men pushed their mounts hard, and when they topped the rise on the west bank of the Hassayampa, they saw that the Mexicans led two packmules up the far side of Richards Crossing.

The marshal piled off his grulla with the trap-door Springfield already in his hand. He'd sighted in the rifle for 500 yards, and the outlaws were at least that far, and moving away.

Havelock bellied down, using his forearms to brace the heavy rifle. He held high, led his target, and gently

15

touched off the big .45–70 slug.

He'd reloaded by the time the report had died away. As he turned the sights on the second outlaw, the first threw his arms wide and tumbled from his mount.

The Springfield roared again. A moment later, the second outlaw's horse stumbled and went down. The rider lit on his feet and ran toward a brush-filled arroyo.

'Now that's shooting,' Reb Carson declared.

'Get that man!' Havelock roared. The four possemen plunged their mounts down the embankment, splashed through the shallow Hassayampa, and struck out after the fleeing outlaw. The mules stopped and began cropping grass along the river-bank. They ignored the shooting and the shouting.

Havelock shoved the Springfield into its scabbard, mounted the grulla, and walked him across the river. The Mexican lay face up, one eye open and staring. The other half of his face had exploded as the Springfield's big slug exited through his right cheekbone. Still, Havelock recognized Innocente Valenzuela from the wanted posters. The one in the arroyo would be Francisco. The brothers stuck together, the dodgers said.

Havelock reined the mouse-colored grulla gelding toward the grazing mules. He wrestled a bullion-box from the first mule and laid it on the waist-high riverbank. He used the steel-plated butt of the Springfield to bang the lock off the bullion-box, hasp and all. He lifted the lid. The box was full of slim golden bars.

*   *   *

A tired, dusty posse rode in just past noon, twenty-four hours after the Vulture Mine robbery.

When the riders turned the corner, a new hangman's noose dangled from the biggest branch of the tough old ironwood. Pappy Holmes stood by the jailhouse door with the Greener in the crook of his arm. Havelock smelled trouble, and his stomach tightened.

'Where's Morgan?' Pappy's rough voice sounded hot and dry as the desert.

'Sent him after Francisco Valenzuela. The Mexican got away.' Wearily, Havelock swung down from the slate grulla.

'Thanks, boys,' he said to the posse. 'Foggarty, take that gold over to the bullion room, would you?'

'Sure, Marshal.'

'Benson, you and Smythe can help him unload.'

The three men rode across the plaza with the two pack-mules and their six bullion-boxes. The other five waited for Havelock to release them.

'That's all boys. Thanks. Oh, Dailey. Can you take my horse over to Wil at the livery? Much obliged.'

The burly rider leaned down for the grulla's reins.

'We're ready to go out again, Marshal, anytime you say. Judd and the super was good men. And we only got two of them what did it.'

'That's good to know, Dailey. Thanks.' Havelock's gratitude was real. How many half-breeds could get that kind of co-operation, and it had been a long time coming, too? He limped into his office, slumped into the chair, and put his game left leg up on the desk.

'Donovan give you any trouble?' he asked.

Pappy squinted at Havelock. He held the 10-gauge Greener like he never wanted to put it down.

'No. Donovan ain't no trouble. It's them law-abidin' townsfolk as wants to hang him 'at's giving me trouble.'

'How'd they find out he's alive?'

'Well, I reckon they figured an old coot like me couldn't never eat enough for two men. Besides, no body ever turned up at the undertaker's.'

'Donovan's still here, ain't he?'

'You ever know Pappy Holmes to lose a prisoner? He's in there. Don't seem worried neither.'

'He'll change his tune when he finds out we got the gold back and one of the Valenzuelas to boot.'

'I'll have to see it.' Pappy turned to peer out the window at the Carrion saloon across the plaza.

Havelock heaved his foot off the battered desk and reached for the ring of keys on the wall.

'Let's go see the prisoner,' he growled.

Donovan lay stretched out on the bunk, hands behind his head. He whistled 'Sweet Betsy from Pike' through his teeth, and didn't look up when the marshal entered.

'How'd it go, 'breed boy?' The outlaw's voice was soft-toned and pleasant.

Havelock stiffened at being called 'breed boy. *Donovan remembers me.*

'Not bad for us, not good for you,' he said, but somehow his words sounded hollow.

'My, my. We seem very confident of ourselves, don't we?' Donovan peered up at Havelock. 'Or are we, 'breed boy?'

'Innocente Valenzuela is dead. Tom Morgan's on the trail of Francisco. And we've got the gold back. Good try, Donovan. You won't get another.' Anger tasted bitter in the back of Havelock's throat. He hacked and spat at the spittoon.

The outlaw's grin grew into a smug smile.

'We'll see, 'breed boy. We'll see.'

'Havelock!' Pappy's bellow came through the thick oak door between the jail and the marshal's office. 'We got trouble.'

'Donovan, people in this town want your hide. But they'll have to come over me to get it. You sit tight.'

'I'm not going anywhere.' Donovan's smile broadened. 'For now.'

Havelock went through the door with Donovan's laughter in his ears. He hated the sound. A twitch of pain shot through his left knee as he twisted around to slam the door.

'What's up, Pappy?'

A fist pounded on the door before Pappy could answer.

'Havelock. Marshal Havelock. It's Belton Phelps. Open up!'

A rumble of angry voices came through the thick door. Havelock held out his hand and Pappy gave him the Greener.

'Back off a step, Phelps. I'm coming out.' The marshal opened the door just wide enough to edge through, shotgun cradled in his arms with the hammers cocked. Havelock raised his voice.

'I don't know what you men figure on doing here but the first one that even looks cross-eyed gets a gutful of BB shot.' He turned to the owner of the Vulture Mine. 'What do you want, Phelps?'

'One hundred thousand dollars in gold bullion.' The florid face of the mine-owner flushed brighter than usual, perhaps from the effort of hauling his 300 pounds and more across the plaza. 'And I want Donovan's neck. I mighta known a Cherokee 'breed didn't have what it took,' he snapped.

Havelock's voice took on an edge.

'You got your gold, Phelps. I saw it myself. Donovan will stand trial. If the judge hangs him, that's fine. But no more necktie parties while I'm marshal of Vulture City.'

'You saw gold, did you? Well, just look at this.' The mine-owner thrust out a golden ingot.

Havelock turned the ingot over in his hand. There, beneath paper-thin gold, a long deep scratch gleamed silvery-gray.

The ingot was lead.

2

Jayzus! Donovan had figured the dumb Cherokee marshal wouldn't be able to spot the hoax. Shit! Havelock handed the counterfeit ingot back to Phelps.

'So that's why Donovan was so smug.' Havelock's voice turned harder. 'Phelps, you can't hang him without a trial. Donovan didn't kill Chambers and Judd.'

'We got a jury, Havelock. Them two's dead, Donovan's alive, and we got us a hanging-tree. Now don't you get in the way, else you get hurt.'

Havelock shifted so that the Greener pointed straight at the belly of the speaker, a black-bearded miner with shoulders that would do Paul Bunyan proud. When Havelock first put on the marshal's badge at Vulture City, a mob of miners had lynched a drifter — just a boy — and Havelock couldn't stop

24

them. He'd sworn then it would never happen again as long as he lived.

'OK, Hunter. Forget all your friends, because there's just the two of us in this. You wiggle so much as your pinky finger, and this Greener will spread your guts all over the plaza.'

The miner stared at Havelock, then swallowed hard. He didn't move. Minus Hunter's bravado, the crowd quieted down and started to melt away.

'You win this one, Havelock,' Hunter growled. 'But even Injuns got to sleep sometime. We'll git that bastard. You count on it.' Hunter stalked back across the plaza to the saloon and banged his way through the batwing doors beneath the sun-baked sign that read CARRION.

'Don't go stirring up trouble, Phelps. I'd hate to have to stop any of your men permanent. But they come after Donovan and you'll find yourself short-handed.'

'I don't give a whit about Donovan, though Chambers and Judd were good men and loyal. I want that bullion.' The mine-owner's priorities were exactly where Havelock thought — gold, first, second, and last.

'Tom Morgan's trailing Francisco Valenzuela. If there's a way to make the Mexican talk, Morgan will know it. He didn't spend ten years with the Apaches for nothing.'

'If the Mex doesn't know, he can't tell. Or, he'll make up some story — Mexicans tell lies from habit.'

'Then don't let Donovan get hung. Dead, he can't say word one about where the bullion is. You'd better have a talk with your boys, calm 'em down a bit.' Havelock nodded at the Carrion, where angry voices suddenly rumbled louder.

'On second thought, Phelps, get out of the way. Those boys in the Carrion are coming and you might get hurt.'

The portly mine-owner scurried across the plaza. As the door of Vulture Mine headquarters closed, the batwings of the Carrion exploded outward and the mob surged through.

'They're coming, Pappy,' Havelock called.

'I'm ready.'

The mob came at a run. Havelock heard Reb Carson's Confederate cavalry yip-yip and Hunter's throaty roar. He let them get half-way across the plaza, then triggered the Greener. BB shot howled into the hard ground a yard in front of the mob. Two men went down, clutching their shins where ricochets hit.

The leaders stopped short but were pushed forward by those behind them. By the time the crowd recovered, Havelock had shoved home two new shells and snapped the Greener closed. The twin clicks of cocking hammers sounded loud in the silence. The mob turned into a group of quiet, confused men who didn't want to look down the barrels of Havelock's shotgun.

This is too easy, Havelock thought. He glanced at the rooflines across the plaza. No one was outlined against the sky, but three second-story windows were open: one in Garth's store, one in the Vulture Mining Company head-quarters, and one in the hotel. Lace curtains in the store window undulated.

The window was too far for the shotgun and a chancy shot with a revolver. The sharp planes of Have-lock's face tightened. He shifted his weight to his good right leg.

'Marshal.' Hunter spoke. 'We'd rather not hurt you. But we're gonna get that crazy Donovan. Chambers and Judd won't rest easy until his carcass swings on the tree, rotted and black. So stand back. There's just too many of us.'

'No there's not, Hunter. We nar-rowed it down before, remember? It's just you and me. You all may have figured out a way to get me, but whatever everyone else does, Hunter, you're a dead man.'

Hunter's face said he didn't like the idea, but his pride wouldn't let him back down.

Someone in the crowd hollered: 'Go!

Do it now. Take him!' The yell triggered the mob.

Havelock took a big step to his right, dropped to his knee, and shoved his back up against the jailhouse wall. A slug plowed into the sun-baked ground on a line with Garth's second-story window. Havelock held the Greener low and triggered both barrels.

Blue smoke, BB shot, and the acrid smell of burnt gunpowder spread from the sawed-off barrels. Several men went down in the street. Havelock drew his Frontier Colt and snapped a shot at the upstairs store window. The bullet ricocheted away with a whine.

From the jailhouse came the roar of the trap-door Springfield. A man crashed through the second-story curtains and fell to the plaza like a sack of grain. His rifle clattered to the rock-hard clay.

Damn. Too many people dying. Havelock levered himself to his feet, holstered his pistol, and broke open the Greener. The crowd rumbled.

'I wouldn't do it, Reb.' Pappy's voice

stopped the lanky Southerner in mid-draw.

Havelock fingered shells into the chambers, snapped the Greener shut, and thumbed back the hammers.

'You all are mighty lucky,' he said. 'No one's dead. Now, throw out your weapons and we'll get Doc Withers to fish the BB shot outta your butts, or wherever else they hit you.'

The men piled their weapons in the middle of the plaza, and Havelock sent a miner for the doctor.

'Get these men in outta the sun.' He waved toward the Carrion. The miners carried their wounded back through the batwings they'd burst from moments before.

When Havelock arrived with Doc Withers, the three men needing doctoring were in the dim saloon. Hunter, with a tourniquet on his right leg, lay on the gaming-table in the rear. Saxbe, a gaunt hanger-on, stretched out on the bar. A third man, a German who spoke almost no English, groaned on a pallet thrown across three chairs. Six other hastily bandaged miners sat waiting. The doctor went straight to Hunter's side, but the marshal stopped just inside the batwing doors. He held the sawed-off shotgun in the crook of his arm, and his face said he'd use the Greener if necessary.

'Hunter, you're a fool,' Doc Withers said. 'You should know better than to rush Marshal Havelock. You could be dead.'

'I know that, Doc. What say you put me back together. I'll repent later.' The big man sounded jovial, but his face was pasty gray. Large drops of sweat beaded his brow. The smell of raw flesh reminded Havelock of fighting blue-bellies at Caulder Mountain.

Doc Withers' eyes narrowed as he cut away the trousers from Hunter's wounded leg. From two inches above the knee to more than half-way up the thigh, it looked like fresh ground beef. But no major artery had been damaged, so the doctor removed the tourniquet. He took a bottle of milky liquid from his satchel.

'Here.'

'What's that?'

'Laudanum. And you'll wish you had more before I get through.'

Hunter clutched the bottle, pulled the cork, and took a big swallow.

'That's enough.' The doctor took back the bottle of narcotic.

The big miner squeezed his eyes shut. His huge frame shuddered. But after a moment, a contented smile came over his face. Then he giggled. Doc Withers went into his leg with a pair of long tweezers. The leg twitched, and the smile left Hunter's face, but he didn't make a sound.

Havelock watched twenty-three BBs come out of the mangled leg before the doctor bandaged it. Hunter went to sleep.

'Pretty well chewed up,' Doc said. 'Still, the tendon's not severed and the bone is OK. He'll limp and it'll be stiff, but I think if he'll work at it he should recover completely.'

The medic went to the other wounded men. Havelock turned to the bartender.

'Send me word when Hunter's awake and can talk.'

'Sure thing, Marshal.' There was a time when the bartender would have said: *No dirty Injuns in the Carrion.* Now he brimmed with good will.

Outside, the plaza baked in the afternoon sun. Havelock wiped sweat from his face with the red bandanna he wore around his neck. He gazed west toward the Big Horn Mountains. *Somewhere out there's a hundred thousand in gold,* he thought. *And on the head of my Cherokee fathers I swear, I'll get it back.*

Inside the jailhouse, the heat hung thick enough to slice. Pappy swiped at his brow with a handkerchief that was more holes than cloth.

'It's about time you showed up, Garet Havelock. A man would think the marshal never comes to his own office.'

Havelock grinned. 'I'm gonna get some sleep, Pappy. You wake me if anything comes up.'

He slept in a little room off the office, and he took his meals at the Gold Skillet, the town's only restaurant. Havelock got the same fare as the prisoners, if there were any in jail.

The marshal pulled his boots off on the bootjack and lay back on the cot. The air was close and stifling, but he fell asleep in an instant, for the first time in nearly two days. And in his dreams, he once again faced Barnabas Donovan.

★   ★   ★

'Red Legs is coming! Red Legs is coming!' Johnny Havelock, Garet's younger brother spread the alarm, and the thunder of hoofs on hardpan soon drowned his voice.

CSA Major Rothwell Havelock, Garet's father, had fallen with Johnston at Shiloh and lay with his men in a mass grave

34

below Bloody Pond.

Marybelle Havelock died of the bloody flux not long after Rothwell. She rested beneath the cottonwood tree with the three baby girls she'd lost.

Johnny, Garet, and an old black woman named Mixie occupied the Havelock home, with Garet nursing half-healed wounds suffered fighting Sherman's army.

For defense they had an old Hawken rifle, a Dance Bros revolver, and a Walker Colt left from Rothwell's Texas Ranger days, before he married his Cherokee sweetheart and moved to the Indian Nations.

'Mixie, you'll want to get out of the house and stay out of sight. These here Yankees may be lookin' for blood.' Garet checked the load in the Hawken, put priming powder in the pan, and pulled back the flintlock hammer. 'Johnny, take the Dance Bros and the extra cylinders. Make yourself scarce. I'll meet the Yankees. Don't you come back 'til they leave, y'hear.'

Johnny pocketed the cylinders, picked up the heavy pistol, and ran through the back door toward the wooded hills beyond.

Garet stepped out the front door to meet the Kansas Red Legs. They rode up in high spirits, like they'd found Rufe Wilkinson's still on the way.

'Howdy, boy.' The captain was big and red-headed, with a reckless gleam in his blue eyes.

'Howdy.' The Hawken was ready.

'And why are you not out with the other Rebel rabble?' The captain seemed to enjoy the sound of his voice.

'Gen'l Watie sent me home. Sherman's boys put me out of the war.'

The captain chuckled. Then he laughed.

'Good.' Then the Red Leg leader's face went hard. 'We have intelligence that Quantrill's raiders are in these parts. Would you have any further information?'

'No, sir.'

'I suspected as much. Still, you would say that regardless of the facts,

would you not? Now, speak the truth.'
The captain's hard blue eyes stared into
Garet's black ones. 'Put down the
flintlock, boy.'

'No, sir. Long as I got my gun, you
die before me.'

Garet felt the cold steel of a Bowie
under his jaw.

'Drop it,' a voice growled in his ear.
He reluctantly lowered the old rifle.

'Rasmussen, Hardy.' The captain
swung off his big horse. 'Bring that boy
down here.' The Yankee walked over to
the big cottonwood that stood near the
house.

Two blue-clad troopers grabbed
Garet by the elbows and turkey-trotted
him over to the captain, who pulled
on a pair of light-colored doeskin
gauntlets.

'I queried you concerning Quantrill,'
he said pleasantly. 'Have you anything
to add?'

'No, sir. I haven't heard and I don't
know.'

Still smiling, the captain drove his

right fist into Garet's gut. The breath exploded from his lungs. The captain's left fist smashed into his nose and blood splattered the doeskin.

The captain drew back his left fist again.

Garet saw the punch coming and dropped like he'd been shot. The captain's fist went over his head to smash into the trooper holding his left arm. The trooper's grip loosened, and Garet tore his arm free. He spun back around to the left until he was behind the other man, his right arm still held in the trooper's big hands. When the soldier followed Garet around, he found a hip in his belly. He flew over Garet's back to land hard on his shoulder.

The captain pulled his Dragoon Colt and cracked Garet above the ear with the long barrel.

Garet regained consciousness to find himself bound to the cottonwood. The house burned and the Red Legs looked ready to leave. Wind blew smoke from the flaming house across the yard and into Garet's nose and eyes. It carried the odour of burning wood and a smell that signaled the end of a way of life.

The captain noticed Garet's open eyes, and reined his bay over to the tree. He gazed at Garet for a long moment.

'You have intestinal fortitude, boy. But we can't have youngsters such as yourself stirring up trouble.' The captain once again drew his Dragoon Colt and cocked the heavy weapon.

'May I ask your name, Captain?' said Garet. 'I'd like to know who killed me.'

'As the frontiersmen say, you have sand, boy.' The captain's smile failed to reach his eyes. He lifted the muzzle of the Dragoon to the brim of his campaign hat in a mocking salute. 'My name is Donovan. Barnabas Donovan. Friends refer to me as Buzz.'

Donovan lowered the Dragoon and shot Garet in the left knee.

*   *   *

Pain woke Havelock. His ruined left knee throbbed as it always did when he failed to get enough rest. Dimly, the clanking of the old piano at the Carrion saloon penetrated Havelock's murky mind. The inside of his mouth tasted of old brass. The backs of his eyeballs burned. The sockets felt full of grit. And the odor of dust and sweat reminded him he'd not washed before going to sleep.

Havelock straightened his leg. The brace squeaked. *Have to tallow that*, he thought. He swung his legs over the edge of the cot, and slipped on a pair of soft elk-hide moccasins. He put one hand on the wall to steady himself, and lunged to his feet.

He scratched a lucifer afire to light the coal-oil lamp, and poured water into the basin from the porcelain pitcher on the commode. The luke-warm water he splashed on his face and neck cut the dust he'd gathered in the desert. The steel razor, stropped on a leather hanging by the cracked mirror, made short work of the sparse whiskers on his dark face. His hair was black with a hint of curl and a touch of gray. The desert sun left crow's feet in the corners of his eyes and scored deep furrows from his nose to the corners of his wide, firmly set mouth. After shaving, Havelock carefully trimmed his full moustache. It, too, showed a sprinkling of gray.

He stripped the red bandanna from his neck and took off his shirt. With a hand towel dipped in the basin and wrung out, he wiped the dust and grime from his muscular torso, pausing once at the puckered scar just below his right collarbone and again at the long one that ran from his left nipple a good twelve inches down toward the point of his left hip, both compliments of Will Sherman's troops.

Havelock continued his toilet, his movements reminiscent of a lithe puma. The brace on his knee was Havelock's design and skillfully made. It supported his joint and worked the same as a real kneecap, allowing the knee to bend forward but preventing it from buckling backward. Garet Havelock with a bum knee was still a lot of lawman.

The marshal pulled on dark brown trousers, donned a shield-front shirt, tied a black silk kerchief around his neck, and strode into the office. As he buckled on his gunbelt, he heard Pappy's clumping footsteps. The latch lifted and the down-home aroma of beef and beans pushed the old man into the room.

'Is that provender I smell?' Donovan's shout came through the thick oak door.

'It's coming. Just hold your horses.' Pappy cast a baleful eye at Havelock and took the prisoner's supper to his cell.

'Jase over to the Carrion said to tell you that Hunter's awake and talking,' Pappy said when he returned.

'I was just going to eat. I'll drop by on my way.' Havelock plucked his

Stetson from the hatrack and picked up the sawed-off shotgun. He opened the door only wide enough to let his lithe six-foot frame through. Quietly he took a long step back and to his right, into the shadow thrown by the eaves. There he paused until his eyes completely adjusted to the night.

The full desert moon bathed the scene in soft silver-blue, concealing the harshness in which the fittest survived by day. To the west, the Big Horn Mountains were a dark shadow against the indigo sky. The stars glittered just out of reach, and the acrid scent of hardy desert growth — mesquite, ironwood, octillo, yucca, and prickly pear — wafted, as tempting as incense.

Havelock took a deep breath and stepped into the street, shotgun in the crook of his arm. Three paces out, he paused. His eyes searched the shadows of the plaza to his left, He looked for anything out of place, any flicker of movement that didn't fit the familiar pattern of Vulture City's night. Before Marshal Melgrade had caught that Jicarilla arrow, he and Havelock had often surveyed the dusty streets together. But now Melgrade was gone, and Havelock, the Cherokee half-breed, wore Vulture City's badge.

Down the other side of the plaza went Havelock's sharp gaze. The reveling inside the Carrion saloon registered faintly on his consciousness, as did the pool of light in front of the Gold Skillet. His relentless eyes flicked from lighted window to shadowed door to dark alley, all the way to the entrance of the Vulture Mine. On this night, all was normal in Vulture City.

A smile played across Havelock's sharp-planed face. Tough and wild as this town was, it was his. Though he was half-Cherokee and a lawman, he belonged. Water had to be wrestled forty miles across the desert from the Hassayampa, but to Havelock, that dollar-a-gallon mud tasted better than sparkling water from a mountain spring.

Inside the Carrion, Jase Bachman led the marshal to a room at the back. Hunter lay on a bed too small for his great body. His trousers were missing a leg and the trunk-like limb that protruded wore bandages from shin to crotch. The antiseptic odour of carbolic acid lingered. The big miner grinned.

'Howdy, Marshal.'

'How ya feeling, Hunter?'

'Think I'm gonna live. I wasn't too sure earlier on today. Doc Withers says it'll take a while to get back on my feet. Says you'd know something about that.'

A hell of a lot more than I want to tell, thought Havelock. He'd spent a year and a half on crutches.

'Yeah, I know,' he muttered. 'But I didn't come over here to swap yarns. I came to offer you a job.'

A man could have driven a twenty-mule team into Hunter's open mouth. At last he stuttered:

'J-j-job? How? I mean, er, what? I

can't do nothing stove up like this.'

'Thing about wounds,' Havelock said, 'the more you use your body, the faster they heal. I want you to guard Donovan. I'll set you up in the other cell and you can sleep there. I'll even provide a shotgun to keep you company. Anyone comes in without singing out, you shoot first and find out who it is later.'

The bearded miner stared at Havelock. Then he threw back his massive head and laughed.

'By God! I'll do it, you heartless Cherokee, and damn me if I don't.'

'Figured you would. Now I can rest easy.' At the door, Havelock turned. 'I'll expect you on the job in the morning,' he said. 'Your pay's thirty a month and found.'

Hunter grinned. 'I'll be there, if I have to crawl.'

3

The stage from Prescott to Phoenix came through Vulture City twice a week. Still, letters were better off sent on the stagecoach than by rider. A lone rider tempted wandering Apaches. Most of the time Indians left the coaches alone. On the other hand, white men robbed the stages every other week or so. Wells Fargo even talked about refusing to carry Vulture's gold.

Pappy and Havelock had just readied Hunter's cell when the stage rumbled in.

'Straighten up a bit, Pappy. I'll go see if the judge is on the stage. It's that time of the month.'

Pappy's retort scorched the air.

Havelock stepped into the blazing morning. His squinting black eyes swept the plaza. The stage stood in front of Vulture Mine headquarters. Wil Jacks backed a new team of four powerful horses into the traces.

A shrill rebel yell split the air and the batwing doors of the Carrion saloon burst outward. Hunter stood there with his arms over the shoulders of Reb Carson and Vernon Mills. Sweat rolled down his pale face and into his beard, which was split by a huge smile.

'Marshal Garet Havelock,' he roared. 'Here I come.'

'I see you, Timothy Hunter,' Havelock roared back. 'And you're late.' The marshal held open the door.

Hunter gave his human crutches a nudge. With his injured leg held off the ground, he hopped across the plaza. The effort drove perspiration from his body in streams, but at last he stood before Havelock, straight and proud, though gasping for breath. He thrust out a huge hand.

'Marshal, I'm reporting for duty.'

Havelock gripped it. 'Come on, then. Start earning your pay.' He took Mills's place at Hunter's left and helped Reb Carson get the big man into the second cell. They settled him on the bed where he sank back for a long moment. Then he heaved his massive torso up and leaned his bulk against the wall.

'Marshal! Where's that shotgun?'

'Right here, you rowdy scoundrel. They's something you'd better learn and learn good. They's only one boss in this here jail, and that's me. John Frederick Holmes, also known as Pappy.' The old man's voice sounded stern, but a smile tugged at the corners of his mouth beneath the white whiskers. 'Take your weapon,' Pappy commanded, and tossed the shotgun at Hunter.

'Hey!' The big man barely managed to catch the deadly gun. 'Be careful with shotguns, will you?'

Pappy ignored him. 'Now, if you'll tell me what kinda cat'ridge you want, you can get that thing loaded and start doing some good around here.'

Hunter cleared his throat to cover his embarrassment.

'Give me half slugs and half BB shot,' he said.

Pappy brought a handful of each. Havelock interrupted the banter.

'Hunter, Donovan's got to stay here until the circuit judge comes around. Skunks out there want him — some to stretch his neck, some to break him loose. You shoot any skunks you happen to see.'

'You can count on me, Marshal.'

'I know I can. Like I said before, if anyone besides me or Pappy comes through door or window, you cut loose with the shotgun. We'll ask questions after we clean up the mess.'

'And Hunter,' Havelock said, 'exercise is good for a wound. So is sleep. You exercise as much as you can. Pull yourself up by the bars. Walk around. But don't you sleep a wink unless you've told Pappy or me first. Y'hear?'

'Marshal, I've been called a lot of things, but I ain't never been called lazy. I'm a man of my word. My old man always said a man's name is only as good as his word. You'll not find a better name than Timothy Hunter. Now you mother hens get out of here and let a man do his job!'

In the next cell, Donovan chuckled at Hunter's speech, but said nothing. Havelock gave Donovan a hard look and left the cell block.

In the office, Havelock spoke to Carson and Mills.

'Boys. I thank you for getting Hunter over here,' he said. 'You showed him he can count on you, and it does a man good to know he's got friends to count on.'

'Marshal,' Reb Carson said, his long hatchet-face dead serious, 'after that boy got lynched, I didn't think much of you and your ways. Seemed to me you leaned on that badge too much. But let me tell you, givin' Hunter a job after he led us crazies across the plaza . . . man, that shines.' Reb blushed under his desert-tanned skin. 'Anyway,' he mumbled, 'if you ever need a hand, just holler. I'm pretty fair with a horse and a gun. I'll ride out again anytime, Cherokee or not.'

The effort of making such a long speech seemed too much for the Texan. He fled across the plaza and into the Carrion.

'You done a right thing with Hunter, Garet,' Pappy said.

'He'll earn his pay.' Havelock went to the window for the umpteenth time. 'Tom Morgan's not back. Either Francisco Valenzuela was tougher than I thought, or Tom's dead. Maybe both. I don't like it. Not one bit.'

'Just you simmer down, Garet. Tom Morgan's as good as they come in the desert. It'd take a heap of *hombre* to kill him.'

Still, Havelock felt uneasy. His eyes kept going to the skyline, though he knew Morgan would never outline himself. Nothing stirred. No breeze. No animal. No bird. No tell-tale dust signaling an oncoming rider. No Tom Morgan.

Night brought no relief. Havelock paced his town with dogged strides, every sense strained toward the desert.

But nothing came out of the darkness.

Long after midnight, Havelock fell exhausted upon his bed without even removing his boots. His dreams were fitful, with a huge black form moving through them like an unwelcome ghost.

Dawn came in delicate rose and coral, bathing the rough stone and adobe of Vulture City with a semblance of beauty. Havelock greeted the rising sun from the outer edge of the plaza. His gaze swept the craggy Big Horn Mountains. Faintly, at the far northern end of the range, he saw Eagle Eye Mountain and the huge hole that gave the mountain its name.

Field glasses in hand, Havelock walked around the jail-house and up the trail to the top of a low hogback. Methodically he searched the desert, and still almost missed the smoke that rose, pencil-thin, between Vulture City and Court House Butte on the far side of Centennial Wash. Havelock squinted at the smoke — could be ten miles away, could be thirty; could be a decoy, could be a signal. Didn't matter, Havelock had no choice but to go.

Havelock dashed for town and almost collided with Jacob Garth, the storekeeper's son, as he turned the corner into the plaza.

'Jake,' Havelock shouted. 'Do me a favor. Run and tell Wil Jacks to saddle up my buckskin horse. Water him good and bring him over to the jail with grain for two days in a gunny sack. Can you do that?'

'Yes, sir, Marshal! Be right back.' The boy ran off and Havelock turned to more urgent matters.

'Pappy,' he called as he came through the doorway. 'I'll be gone for a day or two. You and Hunter keep your eyes peeled.'

'Garet. Don't you go do nothing foolish.'

'There's a smoke down by Court

54

House Butte. It's no camp-fire, and it's not Apache. Probably trouble, but I still gotta go.'

Havelock tucked a snub-nosed pistol into the small of his back where his vest covered it. He slipped a sheathed Bowie knife onto the left side of his gunbelt. It hung over his left hip-pocket. Another knife slid into a sheath sewn inside his right boot.

He plucked a pair of saddlebags from a peg and went into his room. There, he stuffed two pair of moccasins — one soft and ankle-high, the other rawhide-soled and knee-length, Apache style — into the saddlebags, along with an extra Colt revolver.

'Pappy!' Havelock shouted.

'You don't have to yell. I'm right here.'

'Sorry. Would you walk down to Horn Stalker's place and see if you can get me a pound or so of his bighorn sheep jerky. And pick up some corn meal and chili at Jose Mendez's, would you?'

'Sure, Marshal.'

Havelock threw the saddlebags on the desk. He unlocked the gun cabinet and took out a box of .44–40 shells. He filled the empty loops of his gunbelt from the box and dumped the rest in the saddlebag. He slipped five more shells into loops sewn into the crown of his hat.

Havelock cleaned and oiled his pistol and the long-barreled Winchester saddle gun.

'Marshal?' Jake Garth stood in the open door. 'I brung your horse,' he said. 'The buckskin, like you said, Marshal.'

'Let's have a look.' Havelock let the boy through the door first. Havelock eyed the buckskin standing hipshot at the hitching post. He was as good as a desert-bred Apache horse and almost as good as an Apache brave.

'Come with me, Jake.'

'Yes, sir.'

'Who saddled the buckskin?'

'I did,' Jake said, pride in his voice.

'Wil said I could.'

'This ol' buckskin is a little tough to saddle sometimes. So let me show you a trick or two.'

The boy was all big ears and bright eyes. *Be good to have a son like this boy*, Havelock thought.

Havelock slipped his hand beneath the girth. The boy's eyes widened in surprise.

'But. But . . . ' He sputtered. 'The surcingle was tight when I left the livery.'

'Like I said, this ol' buckskin horse has a trick or two. He'll take a deep breath and blow up his stomach so you can't get that cinch tight. What I do is give him a good punch in the belly with my knee. That busts the air out of him.' Havelock smiled at the boy. 'But you're not quite big enough to do that, so you'd better lead the horse around in a tight circle, make him switch head and tail about three times, good and fast. Then take that surcingle up a notch or two, like this.' Havelock tightened the cinch.

'I been meaning to ask you, Marshal. I mean. Well. If you don't mind, sir. Your cinch buckle's on the off side, opposite to everyone else's. I been wondering. I mean. Well, how come, Marshal?'

'You know I walk a bit stiff in one leg, right?'

The boy nodded.

'A man shot me in the left knee one time, and it hasn't worked too good since. I can't get into the saddle from the on side because that shot-up knee won't hold me up. So, to get horses used to me on the off side, I do everything on that side. Cinch up. Mount. Groom. It's kinda made this ol' horse a little odd, though. He thinks his off side is his on side. An ordinary cowpoke had better watch out. This horse comes unwound if someone tries to mount him from the on side.'

'You mind what the marshal tells you, boy. He ain't never talked nonsense in his whole life,' Pappy said. 'You listen to him good and you're liable to live past forty-'leven, like me.' The old jailer chuckled and handed Havelock a bag of provisions and two full canteens.

'That'll be fifty cents for the grub and a dollar for the water, Marshal. Yeah, I know,' Pappy continued before Havelock could answer, 'put it on the books as expenses.'

'That's right,' said Havelock. He tied the sack of provisions over the saddlebags, slipped the Winchester into the saddle scabbard, and mounted the buckskin gelding.

'Pappy. I'm counting on you and Hunter to mind the fort. I won't be gone more than two days. If I can't find out what's going on by then, I'll just turn around and head back.'

Havelock reined the buckskin around the hanging-tree and up the slight incline to the crest of the hogback from which he'd seen the smoke. He took his field glasses from the case that swung from the saddle horn. He focused them toward Court House Butte. The smoke was still there. *Morgan's not coming back,* the thin smoke seemed to say. The smoke grated on Havelock's mind like grit between teeth.

Havelock pushed the buckskin into a ground-eating single-foot, not caring about the dust that rose from its hoofs. The sun passed overhead and dropped toward the rim of the Big Horn Mountains. Three times Havelock stopped to rest the buckskin. Each time, he swabbed its mouth out with his bandanna, wetted from one of the canteens.

He'd decided the smoke came from Burnt Well. *At least the buckskin will be able to drink up before we head back,* Havelock thought, but that's not how things turned out.

The smoke guided Havelock to the well. He saw the fire when he crested the hill. A supply of greasewood sticks were stacked so they'd roll down on the fire as those ahead burned. A fire like that would burn for a good twenty-four hours. Havelock figured this one was set up and lit before dawn.

As he got closer, Havelock noticed

something spitted on a stick about a foot from the fire. He noticed a peculiar smell, too. Something he'd not had in his nostrils since the war — the odor of cooking human flesh.

Havelock squinted against the tears that sprang to his eyes when he recognized the big black right hand of Thomas Jefferson Morgan spitted on a stick, roasting. He didn't stop to put out the fire, and he didn't water his horse, because he could see the stiff legs of Morgan's dead mule sticking out of the well. He just turned the big buckskin and lit out. The fire had turned out to be a decoy and surely Francisco Valenzuela had designs on Vulture City.

⋆   ⋆   ⋆

The buckskin stumbled again, his hide lathered and rough with desert dust, his stride jerky. His great desert-toughened muscles began to fail.

Havelock reined the horse to a stop

61

and swung wearily from the saddle. One canteen was still half-full. He poured the water into his hat and let the buckskin suck it dry. The horse's head raised. He nuzzled Havelock's shoulder.

The marshal hauled the saddlebags and grub sack from behind the saddle, pulled the snub-nosed pistol from his belt, and removed the heavy Bowie knife from his gunbelt. They fitted into the saddlebag after he had removed the long-legged Apache moccasins. He took off his boots and put on the moccasins.

He cached everything in a crevice, sighting landmarks in three directions so he could find them later. He'd make do with Colt and Winchester. He caught up the buckskin's reins and started toward Vulture City.

The sun burned its way to the edge of the Big Horns.

The limping lawman and his game horse struggled toward home. Havelock swallowed, though his throat held no moisture.

The buckskin horse stumbled often, but moved doggedly onward. Havelock sat listless in the saddle, his head bobbing and his tongue swelling.

Man and horse plodded on, relieved somewhat by the evening cool.

Havelock's head snapped up at the unmistakable twin-throated roar of the 10-gauge Greener. Was he that close to town? Adrenaline coursed through his veins. He snatched the saddle gun and slid from the saddle. Sparks of pain lanced through his left knee. He clenched his teeth and ran toward the sound of the shotgun. A pistol barked: one, two, three, four shots. Havelock counted without thought as he plunged onward, rifle at the ready.

The back wall of the jail loomed, and Havelock dropped. He lay still, gasping for breath.

A spark sputtered from the dark shadows to his right. It chased itself in a zigzag line down the jailhouse wall.

'Giant powder!' Havelock roared. 'Pappy. Hunter. Down!' The dry tissues of his throat cracked and tore, and he choked on the welling blood. He spat crimson and dived behind a jutting ledge of desert shale. He pressed his face into the gritty dirt.

The explosion threw dust, rocks, and bits of plaster into the air. The stone wall of the jail threw most of the force of the explosion outward. As the dust cleared, a hole big enough for a man to crawl through appeared in the back wall. A lithe figure in black darted to the hole and hissed: 'Donovan.'

Havelock drew bead on the figure, but before he could call for the man to surrender, a shotgun blast knocked the black figure back, arms wide. The man spread-eagled on the ground, twitched, and lay still.

The marshal struggled up and limped to the corpse. The dead eyes of Francisco Valenzuela were open to the stars, his chest a mass of torn flesh, bloody froth, and strips of black. Now only one robber of the Vulture's gold remained — Barnabas Donovan.

4

The front door to Havelock's office hung awry. A shotgun blast from inside had nearly torn the door from its hinges. Pappy Holmes lay on the floor in a widening pool of blood. He cradled the 10-gauge to his chest. His bleary eyes met Havelock's.

'G-g-garet.' Pappy struggled to speak, his voice old and weak. 'Glad . . . you're back. Couldn't a . . . couldn't a held off that damn Mex much . . . much longer . . . a-a-ahh.' The old man laid his head on his folded arms and died.

Garet Havelock stood very still. From deep in his soul, a bitter smoldering anger arose. With an incoherent roar, he started for the cell block.

At the sound of Havelock's footsteps, Hunter yelled:

'Whoever you are, sing out and sing out now. Elsewise you'll be singing in hell!' Twin clicks of cocking shotgun hammers punctuated the big man's challenge.

'Damn it, Hunter. It's me,' Havelock roared, kicked the door open, and strode to Donovan's cell. The smell of burnt gunpowder overpowered the odor of unwashed prisoner.

'Mark this, Barnabas Donovan, and mark it well. At least three good men are dead on your account. I swear to God in Heaven that I'll see you pay for those lives, in full.'

The redheaded outlaw's voice held a taunt.

'Marshal, you have not one piece of evidence against me for murder. I have killed no one. Besides, what judge or jury's going to take the word of a half-breed Cherokee against that of a white man?'

Havelock frowned. The rage still burned deep inside, but Donovan's smirk and cool attitude helped bank the fire. Havelock took a deep breath.

'Donovan, I owe you. Don't get set

on spending any Vulture gold. Because even if you figure a way out of this jail — and I don't think you will — you keep a sharp eye on your back trail because this Cherokee lawman will track you to hell and gone.'

Donovan smiled again. *Damn his confidence*, thought Havelock. *Damn his Irish gall*.

'Thank you for your concern and undivided attention, Marshal.' Donovan turned to face the wall.

Hunter's cell had a hole blasted in it. Dust covered the bunk and the floor. Hunter's hair and beard were white. His red-rimmed eyes peered from a plaster-dusted face. Two empty cartridges lay on the floor, and he held the shotgun ready. Valenzuela had blown the wrong cell.

'Francisco Valenzuela's dead,' Havelock said. 'An' so's Pappy. We come out on the short end of that bargain.'

'I done the best I could, Marshal. But I couldn't get out of this cell.'

'You done right, Hunter. Donovan's

still here.' Havelock paused, then nodded, his decision made. 'You've got Pappy's job if you want it. He don't have much use for it now,' he said. Havelock didn't wait for Hunter's answer, but he heard the big man say:

'I'll do that job, Marshal, good enough for Pappy and me both.'

The edges of the clotted blood which spread from under the old man had blackened. Havelock turned Pappy over and pried the shotgun from his cold hands. A little smile had frozen on the old man's face. Blood seeped from ragged wounds — one low over the left hip, another through the breastbone.

Townspeople gathered outside the ruined door but Havelock ignored them. At last, Doc Withers spoke.

'Garet,' he said gently. 'Garet. Let us take Pappy away. We'll lay him to rest tomorrow. Let us get him down to Westerly's parlor.'

Havelock looked at the doctor without expression, pain written in his black eyes and across the furrows in his brow.

'Send someone out back to get my buckskin. He carried me far and fast, but we didn't get back in time. Pappy's dead, Doc. Pappy never hurt nothing in his life, Doc, and now he's dead.'

'We're going to take him, Garet. OK with you?'

'Sure, Doc. Take him. We'll bury him in the morning.'

Four men answered Doc Withers's signal. They tiptoed in, picked up the frail old body, and left. Doc Withers stood for a moment longer. Havelock looked up, but said nothing. The doctor stepped toward the battered door.

'You'll find Francisco Valenzuela around back,' Havelock said to the doctor's back. 'He oughta be planted tonight.'

'I'll see to it, Garet,' Doc said. 'You rest.'

Havelock spent the night with his feet propped up on his desk, nodding off and waking, guarding the ruined front door. Hunter didn't rest much better, with a hole in the wall of his cell. Donovan slept like a baby.

The long line of rough men trudged through the streets behind the black buckboard that carried Pappy's casket. The procession started at Westerly's funeral parlor and wound through the plaza and up the hill to the town graveyard.

Pappy's final resting-place was a hole hacked in the desert floor with picks and crowbars. Four men lowered the pine box with two ropes. The rest stood by with their hats off, staring at the open grave.

At last, Havelock broke the silence.

'John Frederick Holmes was a good man. He never let a prisoner get away but he never mistreated one neither. When I get to hell, I hope Pappy Holmes is the jailer.'

Havelock grabbed a shovel and began fiercely scooping clods into the grave. Others joined, trading off with the shoveling until earth mounded above Pappy's meager bones. Someone pounded a wooden marker into the head of the grave. The letters burnt into the slab said:

John Frederick Holmes
1808–1882
Gunned down on the job

The men left, but Havelock stayed on, looking at the grave and seeing the good years he'd spent with Pappy Holmes. Vulture gold put a man in jail, wounded men, killed two mine-workers, two outlaws, and one jailer, and Tom Morgan was missing. *Where is this going to end,* he wondered. *Somewhere out there, there's got to be another man. Donovan and the Valen-zuela brothers didn't do it alone. Else Donovan wouldn't be so cocksure. Bet Donovan figures no Indian boy could ever get the best of him.*

Havelock opened his new front door to find Timothy Hunter sitting in the marshal's chair with his wounded leg propped up on the desk.

'Just because a man's got a scratch or

two don't mean he has a right to my chair,' Havelock growled.

'Yes, sir. No, sir.' Hunter grinned, but didn't move. 'I figured if I've gotta do the work of two men, I'd better start getting around. This here's as far as I got.'

'Good. You just keep up and moving. First thing you know, you'll be worth your salt,' Havelock said.

Hunter's reply was drowned by the rumble of the incoming Wickenburg stage. Havelock walked to the door. The dust settled around the red-and-black-lacquered Concord. Wil Jacks started changing the teams. Four passengers clambered from the coach. Garet recognized the blocky body of M.K. Meade, US marshal, but he didn't know any of the others. His gaze lingered for a moment on the figure of a tall, slim, redheaded woman.

The US marshal came straight to the jailhouse, walking with his head down and body leaning forward. Meade always looked belligerent, though he was a soft-spoken man. With his bowed legs and blocky build, he reminded Havelock of a bulldog. He was just as tenacious, too.

The job of US marshal was a political plum, and many US marshals sat on their duffs. But not M.K. Meade. He did the unpleasant jobs politicos shoved on him without flash or fanfare. Havelock respected the federal lawman. He figured Arizona was the better for the likes of M.K. Meade. Havelock shoved his hand out.

'Morning, Marshal. What brings you to the gates of hell?'

Meade grasped Havelock's hand.

'Garet, m'boy, you really know how to stir things up. Sometimes I think you lie awake nights thinking up ways to make trouble for me.' The tone was jocular, but Meade's face was serious.

Havelock stepped back so Meade could enter the dim office. The heavy door banged shut behind them. Havelock shot a glance toward the cell block. The three-inch-thick door was closed.

Meade looked at Hunter, who sat with his bandaged leg propped up on the roll-top desk, then raised an eyebrow at Havelock.

'Marshal Meade, this here's Timothy Hunter. He's the new jailer.'

'New jailer? Where's Pappy Holmes?'

'Dead. Francisco Valenzuela killed him trying to break Barnabas Donovan out of jail early last night.'

'Make it?'

'No. Valenzuela blew a hole in the wall of the wrong cell a'trying to bust Donovan out. Hunter damn near cut him in half with a sawed-off 10-gauge.'

'Mighta been better if Donovan had of got out,' Meade said.

Havelock made a sharp retort. 'Three good men are dead already because of that man. And the Vulture's out a hundred thousand in gold. If I have anything to say about it, Donovan is going nowhere.'

'Sorry, Marshal Havelock. You'll have to let him go.'

'What!' Havelock's face tightened

down. He wondered what politics were involved this time. Then he noticed the distaste on Meade's face. There was more to the robbery of Vulture's gold than met the eye.

'Garet, the governor's daughter has been kidnapped.' Meade held out a scrap of paper. Havelock took it.

I GOT YUR DOTTER. HAPPEN YU WANT HER LIVING YU GET BARNIBUS DONOVAN TO EAGLE EYE MOUNTAIN IN ONE PIECE. YOU GOT THREE DAYS.

Havelock handed the note back.

The two men stood in silence. Then Meade spoke.

'Garet, you deliver Donovan to Eagle Eye Mountain. As of now, you're my deputy. I need you to do three things, in this order: One, get the governor's daughter out safe; two, bring Donovan and the kidnapper to justice; and three, recover the bullion. No questions asked.' The squat marshal held out his hand. In it lay the simple silver star of a deputy US marshal.

Havelock took a deep breath, letting it whistle out slowly between his big, even teeth. He took the badge.

'How much time?' he asked.

'This is the second day. You gotta be at Eagle Eye Mountain by sundown tomorrow.'

'OK. I'll have the girl in Wickenburg by dawn, day after tomorrow. Then I'll go after Donovan and his partner, and get the gold. That suit you?'

'Be a big help.'

The two marshals had forgotten big Timothy Hunter. He sat silent, moving only his eyes, watching first one lawman, then the other. They stood close together, almost like conspirators. Havelock towered over Meade some six inches, but the disparity didn't affect their attitudes. Their voices were pitched low, their tone conversational. Still, Hunter knew he watched two deadly men.

'Hunter,' Havelock said. 'You heard what Marshal Meade said. I'll be gone however long it takes to do the job. You're in charge while I'm away. As of now, you're Deputy Hunter. I'll put it in writing before I leave.'

'Don't worry none, Marshal. This town will still be here when you get back. I'll see to it.'

Havelock grinned. 'Come on, Marshal Meade. I'll walk as far as the hotel with you. You can get some rest while I get this ballyhoo on the road.'

The two men parted in front of the hotel with a firm handshake. Havelock's attention went momentarily to a striking redhead coming out of the Gold Skillet. She was the same woman as had gotten off the stage with Marshal Meade. He automatically tipped his hat and kept his eyes averted as she swept by with a smile on her face that said she knew who the marshal was even if he didn't know her. That smile stuck in Havelock's mind as he strode down the street toward Horn Stalker's shack.

The wizened Indian squatted in the meager shade of a mesquite arbor. His face was a relief map of the Big Horn Mountains he loved to hunt. Horn Stalker, a Yavapai of indeterminate age, kept the Gold Skillet stocked with fresh bighorn meat. The desert was his home. Even his clothes took on the flat, faded look of the desert at midday — brown, dusty, and entirely utilitarian. Horn Stalker was another of the few men Havelock respected.

'Horn Stalker.' The Yavapai showed no sign he'd heard, but Havelock knew he was listening. 'I'm leaving for Eagle Eye Mountain pretty soon with Barnabas Donovan. I have to turn him loose. Someone on Eagle Eye Mountain has the Vulture gold and the governor's daughter. He'll trade the girl for Donovan.

'I'll take the girl to Wickenburg, so you keep an eye on Donovan and his partner 'til I get back to the mountain. Once the girl's safe, I can bring them in.'

The Indian nodded once, and Havelock knew Horn Stalker would be there when he was needed.

A short time later, four horses stood hip-shot in front of the jailhouse. Havelock was ready, except for the weariness that dragged at his tough body. The hard ride back from Burnt Wells and the fitful sleep of the night before took their toll. Nevertheless, he had to ride, and with Donovan, he could afford nothing less than total vigilance.

'Get up, Donovan. We're leaving.' Havelock opened the iron-bar door to Donovan's cell.

Donovan's smile broadened. 'And where will we be going, Marshal?'

'Eagle Eye Mountain.'

'Well that's just fine.' Donovan smirked.

Havelock pushed Donovan through the open door into the plaza. 'Climb on that bay,' he commanded.

The outlaw mounted. Havelock shackled one of Donovan's hands, ran the chain through the hole in the pommel, and shackled the other. He'd take no chances.

'Marshal, we will be going through Apache territory. I would appreciate a weapon.'

'The note said to deliver you in one piece, Donovan. I'll take care of whatever comes up. You just lie low if there's trouble. And if you need a weapon, you can use that mouth of yours.'

Havelock pulled a lariat from his saddle, built a hangman's noose, and slipped it over Donovan's head, drawing it snug behind the outlaw's left ear.

'Don't make any sudden moves,' Havelock advised. 'This necktie won't get too tight without your doing something foolish.'

Donovan said nothing, but his face lost some of its dare-devil look.

Havelock checked the water in all eight canteens. He slipped a .44–40 carbine into the scabbard on his slate grulla. He put the .50 Springfield in the saddle boot of the spare horse. He took a deep breath and filled his nostrils with the tangy dust of Vulture City.

'Tell Marshal Meade when he comes over that I will meet him in Wickenburg day after tomorrow morning. He'll know what to do.' Havelock said to Hunter, who was standing in the door of the jailhouse.

'Ride careful, Marshal,' Hunter said, sticking out a big hand. Havelock grasped it.

'Thanks. I will.'

Havelock mounted the grulla and picked up the lead lines.

'Come on, Donovan. Time's awasting.'

Havelock halted when Vulture City fell out of sight and sniffed the air. Nothing. He sat for some moments, then set off at a walk. The whiff of dust that had made him stop came again. Someone had moved in the desert just ahead of them.

The Mojave always sharpened Havelock's senses. Maybe its primeval nature whet his Cherokee senses so he noticed and cataloged the normal little goings-on around. So if anything upset that natural rhythm, he noticed it right away.

Havelock rode easy in the saddle, and his eyes inhaled his surroundings. A big horned toad sunned himself on a sandstone ledge. A cactus wren scolded him as he went by, leading Donovan's horse and the two spare mounts in single file.

By now Havelock knew the rider ahead didn't know the desert. And a tenderfoot invited the entire Jicarilla Apache nation to kill. Vulture City lost citizens and visitors to Apaches almost daily. Havelock could personally recall perhaps a hundred who were dead by Apache lance, or worse.

Donovan also noticed the rider's sign. His smug smile widened. Havelock saw Donovan cast about for more sign, and see plenty. An overturned rock. A crushed mesquite twig. The faint smell of acrid desert dust. An outline of a horseshoe in the outer rim of an ant-hill. Sticks scattered from a pack-rat's nest.

The sun crept across the cerulean sky, indifferent to the struggles of those who lived in the desert. Twice Havelock stopped — once to water the horses from the canteens, once to switch mounts.

Eagle Eye Mountain stood a day-and-a-half ride from Vulture City. The note's deadline offered no leeway. Havelock had no time to waste.

But who was the tenderfoot? Who knew what trail Havelock and Donovan would take? Or was Havelock subconsciously following the trail of the rider?

5

Havelock turned the horses toward a spiny ridge west of their course. The lineback dun he now rode picked its way through the cholla, yucca, and prickly pear with ease. A gully in the face of the ridge kept riders and horses off the skyline.

They stopped short of the crest. Havelock walked the dun forward until he could just see over the ridge. There he reined in the dun.

Only Havelock's eyes moved as he searched the trail ahead. Nothing moved. Heat waves shimmered over the desert floor, creating mirages — vast lakes of silvery phantom water — in the distance.

Something moved in the corner of Havelock's vision. He inched his head around until he faced the place where he'd seen the movement. At first, nothing. Then a lithe brown form emerged from a clump of mesquite. Two braves followed the first Apache. Then a fourth. They moved on a straight course, not the zigzag of hunters or the intense caution of those on the warpath. They were homebound. Two of the dusky men had fresh scalps hanging from their belts. From the hair color, the scalps had once belonged to whites. All four Apaches carried US Army issue Springfield carbines.

Their swift dogtrot raised no dust. The braves were spread wide apart, not single file as white men supposed Indians traveled. The four worked as smoothly as trained army scouts, leapfrogging each other, the lead man squatting and searching the terrain while the others passed. *Take a mighty good man to surprise that bunch*, Havelock thought as he watched them out of sight.

The marshal stayed at his look-out long after the Apaches disappeared. Then he backed his horse down to where Donovan waited with the extra mounts — even the outlaw wasn't foolhardy enough to try to escape into the desert. Havelock quickly made the Indian sign for warriors, the sign for Apache, held up four fingers, and then pointed south-west. Donovan nodded. He held up his manacled hands with a question on his face. Havelock shook his head. He took up the lead rope to Donovan's horse, gathered in the loose end of the lariat attached to Donovan's neck, and moved north-west at a slow walk.

Still, Havelock felt uneasy. Four Apaches meant more Apaches, and any Apache meant trouble. Havelock didn't like it. The tenderfoot up ahead would draw the Jicarilla like a corpse draws flies.

The heavy roar of a Springfield signaled the start of a fracas. Two more shots followed close behind, then the feisty bark of a Winchester saddle gun.

The fight lay dead ahead, about half a mile away by the sound.

Havelock turned west toward high ground. Desultory firing continued as he led Donovan and the extra mounts in a wide circle. He stopped when the shots sounded due east. A hogback hid the fight from him.

'I'm going over there for a look-see,' Havelock whispered. 'You'll be here when I get back if you're smart.'

'You go right ahead, Marshal. Pay me no mind.' Donovan's words carried bravado, but he kept his voice low.

'On second thought, I think I'll play it safe.' Havelock walked around to the side of Donovan's horse, taking up the slack in the rope around Donovan's neck as he went. He cocked his Winchester and shoved the muzzle under Donovan's chin. The outlaw strained away from the deadly gun. Keeping up the pressure, Havelock unlocked the shackle on Donovan's right hand.

'Step down slow and easy.'

Donovan dismounted.

'Sit down with your back to that mesquite.'

Donovan sat.

Havelock took the chain around the slim tree, pulling Donovan's left arm behind his back and around the tree-trunk. Then he pulled the chain over the outlaw's stomach to fasten to his right wrist. Now he'd stay put.

'Thanks for leaving me to the fowls of the air, boy.'

'You stay real still and the buzzards won't even notice you're around.'

Havelock led the horses almost to the top of the hogback, where he tied them in a clump of scrub oak. They'd keep to the shade, out of sight.

The thought of crawling brought a twinge to Havelock's game knee, but had to be done, so he crawled.

Sporadic firing continued. The Springfields seemed to change position, but the shots from the Winchester always came from the same place.

At last, Havelock looked down on the battlefield. A chestnut sorrel horse lay down and dead. A flicker of movement behind it said the rider was still alive.

With the flicker, a Springfield spoke. Havelock spotted the Apache by the smoke from his carbine, an older man, black hair liberally streaked with gray. A calico headband kept his long hair in place.

One.

Movement off to the left showed Havelock the second Indian. A youngster on his first sortie, perhaps. The boy sneaked around to flank whoever took cover behind the dead sorrel. The boy was good, but not good enough to escape the notice of a Cherokee.

Two spotted. There should be another.

But Havelock couldn't spot him. Besides, that youngster was getting too close. The boy jumped up to make his dash, a *netdahe* war whoop on his lips, and Havelock killed him. Instantly he shifted his aim toward the older man, but the Apache was no longer there.

The third man's bullet kicked dirt and bits of desert rock into Havelock's face. Havelock rolled frantically, disregarding the sharp prickles of cacti.

Two full turns and he was up on his elbows, rifle at his cheek, aiming at the place from which the shot had come.

At first he saw nothing. Then a small bird, about to land on a patch of cholla, suddenly veered and flew to another landing place further on. Havelock put seven shots into the clump as fast as he could work the lever, spacing the shots evenly across its width. A moccasined foot pushed its way into sight, digging a furrow in the desert dust. It arched stiffly, quivered, and went limp. The warrior had not made a sound.

Havelock waited. The foot did not move. He lifted his gaze to the place where the boy went down. The body was gone!

The sound of hoofbeats came from a gully on the far side. The old Apache boiled over the edge, going away. The old man held the body of the boy in front of him across the withers of his pinto pony. Could be his son, Havelock thought, or maybe his grandson. He let the old man go.

A red-headed woman stood up from behind the downed sorrel. Havelock stared. He'd seen her near the Gold Skillet, where she'd given him that knowing smile.

Havelock struggled to his feet, and nearly met his maker. When he looked at the redhead again, she had her rifle to her cheek, aimed at him.

Dimly he heard the report of the rifle. His head split into a million pieces of blinding light. As he fell he wondered: *why? Why would that woman shoot me?*

* ⋆ ⋆ ⋆

The first thing Havelock heard after the rifle shot was the agonized death squeak of a pack-rat, followed by the near-silent flurry of beating wings as a night predator bore its prey away. He started at the sound, and pain seared through his head. He lay motionless. The pain dulled.

Slowly, he opened his eyes. He

remembered. The redhead from the Gold Skillet had shot him. Late afternoon. Now night.

Donovan. He'd left Donovan shackled to a tree. Havelock turned over. He lay motionless until the pain dulled again. He fell back three times while trying to get up on all fours, but the pain in his left knee told him crawling would never work.

Twice he attempted to stand. Both times he awoke stretched full length on the ground. Pain flashed through his brain. He started inching his way to where he'd left Donovan, dragging his left leg straight out behind.

Havelock found the tree, but Donovan was gone. Then he realized the horses were gone, too. He'd struggled past the scrub-oak thicket without noticing. And his predicament hit him full force.

No horses.

He checked his holster.

No gun, though the belt held bullets. The snub-nosed pistol he usually carried in the small of his back was still cached near Burnt Wells, along with his big Bowie knife.

The woman had taken his guns, but not his boots. Fighting the red mist of pain that seared his brain, Havelock managed to extract the thin, razor-sharp stiletto from his boot — his only weapon, and his only tool.

With the knife, he cut a branch from the mesquite tree, trimmed it to about six feet long, so one end was about the thickness of his wrist and the other slightly larger than the base of his thumb. The branch was crooked, but it would have to do.

Grasping his new staff as high as he could reach, Havelock pulled himself to his feet. For a long moment he stood still, panting, as his head reeled and his stomach heaved. Cautiously, he raised a hand to his head. His fingers explored hair matted with dried blood, then found a furrow the redhead's bullet had plowed across his head, starting about two inches above his left ear. If he'd not been falling away . . .

The woman had not killed him, and *that was her big mistake*, Havelock thought. *She just doesn't know the stubborn nature of an Oklahoma Cherokee.* He'd promised to free the governor's daughter. He'd promised to bring in Donovan, dead or alive. And he'd promised to get the gold back. Even half-breed Cherokees kept their promises.

Havelock took a tentative step. The insides of his head rattled, but didn't get any worse. Gingerly, he walked to where he'd tied the horses. Even in the moonlight, he could read the sign. Donovan and the redhead had ridden the horses north-west toward Eagle Eye Mountain.

Hobbling to the place where he'd been shot, Havelock found his hat off to the right. The five .44 bullets he habitually carried in the crown were still there. His spirits picked up. There might be a way out of this mess yet.

Still leaning heavily on his mesquite

staff, Havelock made his way to where the second Indian had fallen. The brave was still there, stiff in rigor mortis. No one had come back for him yet. Havelock knew he had to get away quickly, and had to stay out of sight, or his hair would festoon an Apache war shirt.

The dead Apache clutched an old Springfield. Havelock broke the hammer. He took the long knife from the Indian's belt. It wasn't a Bowie, but it was good and sharp.

Using more strength than he knew he had, Havelock turned the stiff corpse over, and the handle of a Colt revolver protruded from under the dead brave's vest. He seized it and pulled it out. Even in the starlight, Havelock recognized an old cap-and-ball Dragoon that had been converted to cartridges. It was fully loaded. Havelock removed one cartridge, rotated the cylinder so that the empty chamber lay beneath the hammer, and thrust it into his holster. He shoved the bullet into an empty loop on his gunbelt. The familiar weight of a weapon at his hip made him feel better.

Now, if that blasted thirst that turned his throat to sandpaper would just go away, he'd be all right. *But it won't*, he thought. *The thirst'll get worse. Much worse. My tongue'll turn black. I'll scorch. I'll go crazy and chase after mirages.* Havelock knew that living hell would come over the horizon with the rising sun.

A thought hit Havelock. She'd shot him late in the afternoon. Likely the woman and Donovan would not have gone far before camping for the night. Especially if they thought Havelock was dead. Maybe he could spot their camp-fire from the hill behind him.

Havelock got up the hogback quicker than he'd imagined he could, and when he got there, his head throbbed less, though nausea still twisted his innards.

Despite the tough climb, Havelock didn't sweat. The dry desert air and loss of blood from his wound had robbed his body of too much moisture for him to perspire.

Taking his bearings from the waning moon, Havelock first located the dark bulk of Eagle Eye Mountain in the distance. He searched the desert floor with careful eyes. There! Fire. Reflected off a sandstone face among the foothills on the left.

That's smart, he thought. *Don't make a beeline for the mountain. Keep to the foothills where you can stay out of sight.*

The fire had to be Donovan's. Had to be. He'd go there, he decided. And with luck and enough strength, he'd get there before sunrise.

Before leaving, Havelock went back to the dead Indian and removed the brave's knee-high moccasins. He sat down, took off his boots, and tried the moccasins on. They were a bit loose, but much better than cowman's boots for hiking across the desert. Havelock tied the leggings over his trousers, left his boots by the dead Indian in exchange, and struck out toward the dim reflection of camp-fire.

* * *

Back in Vulture City, Timothy Hunter, deputy marshal's badge pinned to his vest, made the rounds. His progress was slow, he leaned heavily on a knotted cane, but no one thought of arguing with the sawed-off shotgun in the crook of his arm, or with the set look of determination on his bearded face.

In a Jicarilla Apache rancheria deep in the Big Horn Mountains, a huge black man with a missing right hand rested quietly, his fever broken at last.

* * *

The moon set, leaving the land flat and black. A red haze burned behind Havelock's eyes as he plodded toward the flicker of light.

The light edged closer. The reflection weakened as the fire died, but now

Havelock was close enough to catch even the faint glow of coals giving up their last glimmer of life.

The need for caution invaded his numbed and throbbing brain. He stopped, shoulders hunched, swaying back and forth like a grizzly scenting the wind. His eyes had sunk deep into the dark sockets of his face. His lips had thinned down, raw edges to the wound that was his mouth.

Weariness sucked at every cell in his body. Every scrap of tissue cried for moisture. With infinite care, he lifted the heavy old Dragoon Colt from his holster. The left hand followed the right to the grips of the old gun, for Havelock needed two hands just to raise the pistol. With both thumbs, he cocked the hammer. The click sounded like a rifle shot in the ink-black silence.

Havelock stood for a long moment, listening. No flurry of movement, no unnatural sound, followed the cocking of the pistol. Off to his left he heard the patter of pack-rat feet. Further on a beetle clicked.

Havelock worked closer to the edge of the clearing. The fire now held hardly a glow. In the deep shadows next to a bluff rising behind the campsite, Havelock could make out two prone forms. *Got 'em*, he thought, and gathered his strength for the encounter.

With a deep breath, he took three long steps into the clearing and faced the forms.

'All right, Donovan. You're covered.'

The prone forms remained motionless, mocking the half-breed Cherokee. Bitter bile rose in Havelock's throat, choking off his oaths. For the second time in three days, he'd followed a decoy fire.

The shaking began deep down in his guts. It was like ague, only worse. A chill swept through his body. His teeth chattered out of control. He sank to his knees, then toppled over on his side. Inside his head, the fires of hell raged. He blacked out.

The sun was high when Havelock awoke, far into the day he was to deliver Donovan to Eagle Eye Mountain in exchange for the governor's daughter. He stared for a moment at the cobalt blue of the morning sky. Suddenly, he sensed a presence. He carefully turned his head to look across the dead ashes of the decoy camp-fire. An Indian squatted patiently in the shade of a clump of organ pipe. Havelock grimaced to notice that the circle of ashes from the camp-fire was a good six feet across, much too big for a camp-fire in hostile Indian territory. He hadn't noticed that the night before.

Havelock tried his voice. 'You wouldn't have a drink on you, would you, Horn Stalker?' he said in a coarse cracked whisper.

The Yavapai got up and padded over to the fallen lawman. Without expression, he stared down at the marshal. Then he smiled.

'What would you do, lawman, if I

weren't around to get you out of these messes?'

'Guess I'd have to locate another educated Yavapai to be my friend.' Havelock's attempt to smile cracked his lower lip, allowing a dark drop of blood to ooze out. He was too dehydrated to bleed much.

Horn Stalker knelt in the dust and uncapped his canteen. First he wet a bandanna and held it to Havelock's face. The marshal sucked greedily at the damp cloth. Tiny trickles of life worked their way down his throat. The water was brackish and lukewarm. Havelock had never tasted anything better in his life.

He reached for the canteen. One sip. Two. A delicious coolness spread through his parched body. Layer upon layer of tissue revived with each swallow of water.

Then Horn Stalker spoke again, this time seriously.

'Apaches are not far away. They follow from the body of the brave you killed yesterday. It will be a close thing as to who gets to Donovan first, us or the Apaches.'

The lithe old hunter disappeared into the desert flora surrounding the clearing. In a moment he reappeared leading two horses. One was Havelock's grulla, saddle, Winchester, and all.

'I found him headed back to Vulture City. There wasn't no one around so I claimed him as a maverick. You happen to know who he belongs to? Damn fine horse.' Horn Stalker's obsidian eyes sparkled.

'Anyone who tries to get on that horse from the on side gets dumped, quick,' said Havelock. 'I trained him that way myself. Glad I did, too.'

Havelock got to his feet with only two attempts. Horn Stalker did not offer to help, nor did Havelock ask. Both knew the unwritten law of the desert said a man either took care of himself, or died.

Havelock limped to the grulla. He gathered the reins, lifted his right foot and pushed it into the off-side stirrup. Grasping the saddle horn with both hands he heaved himself aboard the patient horse. He sat a moment while his head cleared. Then he looked at his Indian friend.

'Let's ride.' he said.

Horn Stalker nodded, and led off on a trail toward Eagle Eye Mountain which no white man had ever followed before.

A fast single-foot pace soon brought the two desert riders to the foothills of the Big Horn range. Eagle Eye Mountain towered to the north, its baleful single eye — a hole that ran completely through the mountain near the summit — just visible.

The Yavapai picked his trail carefully. Even an Apache would make slow going of it. The signs were few. Both Horn Stalker's and Havelock's horses had rawhide boots instead of iron shoes. They left precious little in the way of tracks. In fact, a white man would probably have sworn no horses had passed that way.

The Apaches seemed to materialize right out of the ground. One moment the desert was quiet and peaceful, the next it was shattered by gunfire.

Havelock palmed the old Dragoon by reflex. He stuck it in the nearest Apache's face and pulled the trigger. It seemed like an eternity between the click of the descending hammer, the roar of the old .44, and the destruction of that wild Apache face. Now, at least, he knew that the old gun would actually fire.

'Ride!' Horn Stalker's shout registered dimly on Havelock's consciousness. He sent another bullet after a shadowy desert form but couldn't tell if it did any damage. Then the two riders burst through the line of Apaches and thundered on toward Eagle Eye Mountain.

From behind them came the whoop of pursuing Apaches. No longer any need for silence now, and the desert guerrillas liked a good chase.

'I know of a cave on the side of Eagle

Eye Mountain,' shouted Horn Stalker. 'We could make a stand there.'

Havelock nodded. He also noticed a red stain spreading from beneath Horn Stalker's left arm, and the gray cast of the Yavapai's face. But he was a hard man. He'd do what had to be done. And Havelock would stick with him.

'How far?'

'Soon. If we can hold the pace.' Horn Stalker didn't look like he could go ten paces, much less miles. Yips from the pursuing Apaches sounded closer.

Shots began to buzz by the fleeing horsemen. Random shots they were, but a lucky random shot can kill a man as dead as a well-aimed one.

Horn Stalker's hand lifted. He made sign language for 'Not far. Hurry,' and pointed to a scar on the side of the mountain. Havelock nodded.

The grulla grunted and broke stride. Then he settled back to his old rhythm for a few moments.

Fifty long strides the grulla took, putting all the effort left in his dying heart to carrying Havelock up the slopes of Eagle Eye Mountain. Fifty long strides, and the grulla collapsed, dead before he hit the ground.

Havelock had time only to slip his feet from the stirrups and snatch the Winchester saddle gun from the saddle boot. Upon impact he was rolling, frantically seeking shelter behind the dead horse before the Apaches caught up with him. He came to a stop with the rifle pointed back the way he had come. He took a deep breath and waited for death to come sneaking in from the desert.

6

Horn Stalker's horse carried him up and over the lip of the rise that fronted the cave. *At least likely he'll make it,* Havelock thought.

Suddenly, only the sound of Havelock's harsh breathing broke the sunbaked silence. A bluetail blowfly buzzed at the blood oozing from a hole low in the dead grulla's abdomen. More bluetails joined the first. A big yellow jacket arrived, but no Apaches came.

Havelock remained motionless. Sweat formed under his hatband and stung in the furrow from the redhead's bullet. It rolled down his brow, and it trickled along the valley between his shoulder blades. He now breathed shallow and soundless. His unblinking black eyes stared straight down the trail, though he knew the Apaches would come from the sides. Long ago, when he was a lad in Oklahoma, his Cherokee grandfather had taught him a man can spot small movements better with peripheral vision.

Let 'em come, Havelock thought. *Today's as good a day to die as any.* He gritted his teeth against the throbbing pain in his head. He fought the urge to move, to lessen the pressure on his bum knee, to find a more comfortable position. He wondered if he should compose a death song.

A rifle cracked from the lip of the rise about twenty feet from where Horn Stalker's horse had disappeared. An Apache brave arched from behind a creosote bush, clawing at his torn throat. Sounds of the warrior's thrashing faded. The desert turned silent again.

A flicker of buckskin against the desert caught the corner of Havelock's eye. He didn't turn his head, only his eyes. Havelock saw nothing, but he knew an Apache hunkered there. He coiled his muscles, ready to meet the Jicarilla attack.

They came from three directions.

Havelock had already aimed at the warrior who rose from behind a clump of tumbleweed. The Winchester seemed to move of its own accord, lining up on the Indian's broad naked chest. Havelock squeezed the trigger. The 200-grain slug dusted the Apache front and back. He flopped to the desert floor, dead.

Havelock didn't watch the body fall. He swung the rifle to meet the rush from straight ahead. Two warriors came, one big and burly, the other wiry and dried as if his muscles were made of jerky. Havelock picked the smaller target and pulled the trigger.

The thin man spun about and went down as Havelock jacked another shell into the Winchester's chamber. Havelock heard firing from the lip of the rise, from more than one rifle. He shifted his aim toward the big brave, but the Apache had disappeared.

Again silence fell on the slopes of Eagle Eye Mountain. Havelock didn't move. The Apaches might have gone, but then again they might be just lying low. Apache netdahe braves have the same aversion to lead poisoning as any man.

'Iron Knee,' called a voice from beyond the lip.

'I hear you, Horn Stalker.'

'The Apaches have gone, my friend. Come.'

'All right.' Havelock stood up, gingerly flexing his left knee. He limped around the dead horse to where he could loosen the girth and strip the saddle from the grulla's back. With a toneless curse, he started up the slope with the heavy saddle slung over his shoulder.

Havelock climbed with his Winchester in his right fist, loaded and cocked. Horn Stalker had used Havelock's Indian name to warn him all was not as it seemed, and he'd heard more than one rifle firing.

The muzzle of the Winchester came over the edge of the rim first, topped by Havelock's watchful black eyes.

'Come on up, Cherokee boy. Join our little party.' The cold light in Donovan's blue eyes didn't match his jovial tone of voice. 'Everyone is present and accounted for. Let me make introductions.

'That old Red Indian lying on the blankets is Horn Stalker, sometime employee of the marshal of Vulture City and hunter for the owner of the Gold Skillet of the same metropolis. The woman tending him is my sister, Laura Donovan.'

'Half-sister,' the woman said.

'We've met,' Havelock said, deadpan.

The woman ignored Havelock and continued working on Horn Stalker's wound with a sure but gentle touch. *She's seen and treated wounds before. She'll do*, Havelock thought.

Donovan took in the angle of Havelock's hat, perched on his head to avoid the crease Laura Donovan had put in his hair. The smile on Donovan's face came close to a sneer as he said:

'Yes. I see you have met. Laura is an

excellent shot. I'm surprised you are still with us.'

'Cherokee luck.'

Neither Havelock nor Donovan mentioned the Winchester that Havelock held fully cocked and casually pointing in Donovan's direction. A shooting here would only help the Apaches come out on top.

A young cowboy with gold-red hair emerged from the shadows of the cavern. His wide blue eyes gave him a look of youthful innocence, furthered by the grin on his face. The freckles scattered across the bridge of his nose made him look young, but he wore a man-sized Colt that showed signs of frequent use. Havelock decided the youngster was someone to steer clear of in a scrap.

Donovan took the younger man by the arm.

'This is my baby brother, Archibald Donovan,' he said to Havelock. 'Finally got all my family together. First time in more than ten years. I suppose I've got you to thank for that, Cherokee boy.'

'Me, I'm his half-brother, like Laura's his half-sister,' the youngster said, still grinning. 'We got the same pa, but different mas.'

Havelock could not have cared less. 'Where's the girl?' he demanded, his voice cold and sharp.

'She's all right. Don't you worry none. May be a problem, though. Seems she don't want to go back to that stodgy pa of hers. She likes it right here with the likes of us.'

Archibald Donovan turned toward the mouth of the cavern.

'Come on out, Carrie honey. He won't hurt ya.'

Marshal Meade had called her a kid, and the girl who came out of the cave might have been no more than fifteen years old. But in every other way she was a woman.

The girl wore men's clothes, and they were a little big on her. But her well-formed breasts pushed at the shirt fabric, and her full hips filled the jeans.

The outfit probably came from the younger Donovan's warbag. She twined her arms about his waist and lifted her face to him. Naturally, he kissed her.

'The deal was the girl for Donovan,' Havelock said.

'Arch, let go of that child,' Donovan ordered.

The young man reluctantly complied. He turned to Havelock.

'Marshal, I'm more than willing to keep my word. In fact, I make a point of doing that. Only thing is, I don't like to force folks to do what they don't want to.' He faced the girl and continued; 'Carrie don't wanna go back to Prescott, do you, honey?'

The girl shook her chestnut curls negative. She had not spoken a word, and that bothered Havelock. But before he could question her, a shot from the desert sent everyone scrambling for cover. From the corner of his eye, Havelock noticed that the girl had not moved at the sound of the shot. She followed a second later, reacting to

Arch Donovan. The delay troubled Havelock for a moment, then staying alive took top priority.

The height advantage of the small clearing in front of the cave kept the group alive. For the first five minutes, with the roar of gunfire sounding more like a war than a battle. Havelock glimpsed Laura Donovan down on one knee, using her long-barreled saddle gun with quiet efficiency, and he realized that back in the desert her shot had not gone astray by accident. If she'd wanted, he'd be fodder for the buzzards. He couldn't help but wonder why she'd pulled up.

The Apaches dropped back with a warrior dead and perhaps two wounded. Five sets of eyes, two black and three blue, searched the desert for signs of Apaches. The hot sun reached the tops of the Big Horns and began to slide around the edge of Eagle Eye Mountain. And out on the flat, a spot of sunlight stood out in the sun-cast silhouette of the mountain: the eye of the eagle.

'Looks like they have gone,' said Donovan, easing back from the edge of the rim.

'They'll be back.' Havelock said.

'Once more before the sun leaves,' said Horn Stalker.

Donovan's face darkened with anger. He seemed used to people agreeing with his opinions.

'I am not unfamiliar with Indian warfare. I have fought Apaches in the past. And I say they will not come again today.'

Maybe the Apaches themselves decided to make an ass of Barnabas Donovan. The first shot sent Donovan's greasy Stetson flying and its owner diving for cover. The second showered sharp bits of sandstone into Havelock's face, narrowly missing his right eye and drawing tiny droplets of blood from his cheek.

'Marshal!' The warning came from Laura Donovan. Havelock squeezed off a shot and rolled sharply to his left, knowing as he did that his shot had missed. As he faced upward he saw what the woman had warned him of. A blocky Apache brave had come down the mountain from above the cavern. Havelock barely had time to take the chopping war axe on the wooden forearm of his rifle, which stopped the blade inches from his face. Havelock put his right foot in the brave's belly and pulled on his rifle. The Indian went up and over Havelock's head, landed on the downhill side of the lip, and tumbled down the incline.

Havelock rolled another half-turn to the left. The brave he'd missed before was near the top of the slope. Havelock felt the cold certainty in his gut that said he didn't have time to shoot. Still he tried to bring the Winchester into play. The Apache's victory cry became a gurgle and he fell heavily atop Havelock, splashing the marshal with blood. Havelock shoved the body aside, not looking to see who had shot the warrior; he knew Laura Donovan had done it.

'Buzz, I've only got three more rounds,' Arch said.

'Laura?' Donovan asked.

'Two,' she said.

'Red man?'

'Three,' said Horn Stalker through clenched teeth.

'Cherokee?'

'Two in the rifle and three in my pistol,' Havelock said, his voice scratchy from breathing gunsmoke. He kept the five cartridges in the crown of his hat as trumps.

'Havelock. Garet Havelock.' A deep voice called from the desert.

'Tom Morgan! I hear you.'

'Come down here. Let's parley.'

Havelock stood up. He took a step forward but the loud click of a cocking hammer stopped him.

'You will not leave this area,' Donovan said. 'I do not trust that black Indian and I do not trust you, white Cherokee. You will stay.'

Laura Donovan cocked her rifle and held it on her brother.

'Let him go. He may be the only one who can get us out of here. If you so much as twitch, Buzz, I will personally blow the back of your head off. In Vulture City people said Marshal Havelock kept a mob from hanging you. He could have let them have you, you know.'

Donovan didn't like it, but neither did he want to test Laura's word.

'He wanted the Vulture gold,' Donovan rasped. 'That's all.'

'I don't think so, Buzz. I heard a lot of talk in town that said the marshal's honest. I believe it.'

'There's no such thing as an honest Indian, especially half-breeds,' Donovan growled.

The woman's eyes stayed on Donovan. 'Marshal, if you go out there, will you come back?'

'Of course. I've got a job to do. I'm supposed to return the governor's daughter. I'll be back.'

'Then go.'

Havelock looked into Laura's eyes for a long moment. Then he nodded, stepped off the rim, and carefully picked his way down the slope. His rifle drooped casually from the crook of his right arm.

Fifty yards from the lip, two warriors materialized in front of Havelock. He stopped, rifle ready. They signaled him to follow and walked away through head-high stands of cholla.

Havelock passed through the cacti as deftly as the Apaches. Two more painted men closed in behind him. He wasn't comfortable, but he didn't let it show. He held his face as expressionless as if he were out for a Sunday stroll.

The desert opened up into a large clearing. A huge gaunt figure lay on a pallet, his right arm ending in a well-bound stump. The old Indian Havelock had seen riding away from the firefight stood at Morgan's side.

'Howdy, Tom.' Havelock's voice was neutral but his eyes showed concern for his friend. He ignored the old man.

'Passable, Garet. Passable. You should have told me those Valenzuela boys was half-Yaqui. I'da been a heap more careful. Us Apaches don't even cross a Yaqui's back trail without mighty good cause.'

'Had I known, you'da been told.'

Morgan changed the subject. 'Some pickle you've got yourself into. What's the deal?'

Havelock quickly filled him in. 'Ordinarily I would have sent you out to arrange a safe passage through this territory,' he said. 'As it was, I had to bungle through on my own. There are six of us up there: three whole men, another wounded, and two women, one of whom can shoot better than most men.'

Morgan listened to Havelock. His paper-thin skin pulled tight against his skull. His eyes peered from hollows under craggy brows. Dark crevices beneath his cheekbones spoke of the ordeal he had survived. But now, he was concerned for his friend.

'Too bad you killed that boy, Garet. He was the grandson of the old chief here.'

'I figured something like that. Otherwise they wouldn't keep coming like they do. How do we get around it?'

'Don't know if you can.'

'Iron Knee.' The strong voice of the old man standing next to Morgan held authority. 'Only you. You stay. Others go. Tomorrow you run. My warriors will kill you. Your life for the son of my son.'

'I guess that's it, Garet. If you surrender, they'll let the others go. I talked them into not killing you outright. You get to run. It's a thing Apaches do for brave enemies.'

Havelock had no choice. His first duty was to get the governor's daughter safe to Wickenburg. If his surrender would free the others, fine. At least he'd have a running chance . . . even if he was a Cherokee half-breed with an iron knee.

'Thanks, Tom. A running chance is all a man can ask for.' Garet turned to the chief. 'Grandfather,' he said, 'I would that your grandson had not died by my bullet. But he did, so I will run against death. I shall go to those in the cave and tell them to leave. I return in the middle of night. Tomorrow I run.'

A flicker of something that might have been respect crossed the old man's face. He nodded curtly and turned his back on Havelock and Morgan.

Havelock grasped the left hand Morgan held out to him.

'I'll be back shortly,' he said. As he retraced his steps to the cave, he wished the throbbing in his head would go away.

At the cave, Laura Donovan kept watch, rifle in hand. Havelock caught a flicker of fire in the recesses of the cavern, and smelled cooking meat. His stomach rumbled, reminding him that he'd not eaten since before noon the previous day.

Havelock held his face expressionless, then smiled at Laura, but not with his eyes. He walked toward the cave. He paused at the cave's mouth, but didn't look back. Then he squared his shoulders and stepped inside.

Arch and Carrie held hands, sitting on the far side of the fire. Donovan tended a large chunk of spitted meat that sizzled over the flames. A pot of coffee steamed in the coals at the edge of the fire, filling the cave with an aroma that complemented the smell of roasting meat. Horn Stalker lay on a saddle blanket against the cave wall.

Donovan looked up.

Havelock raised his eyebrows at the meat.

'Arch got an antelope yesterday morning,' Donovan said.

From the darkness beyond the firelight came the restless stomp and rustle of horses picketed back in the cave where Apache horse stealers could not get at them. Havelock heard Laura walk in behind him.

'What happened?' Donovan's voice showed his contempt for Havelock. 'Did you sell us to that black Apache to save your hide? What kind of deal are you two working against us now?'

'Donovan, one of these days you'll jump to a conclusion that will get you killed. So shut up and listen.' Havelock's Winchester pointed at Donovan's big hard stomach, and he thumbed back the hammer to emphasize his point.

'Don't be disturbed, Marshal. Hold your temper, now.' Donovan said, holding up a placating hand.

Havelock let the silence hold. Then he spoke.

'Arch, it's time to quit funning. Do you think as much of Carrie as you've been saying?'

'Yes, sir, Marshal. I do.'

Havelock then spoke to the girl, but kept his eyes on Arch. 'What about you, Carrie? Do you want to stay with Arch?'

The girl said nothing.

'Marshal, she can't answer you. She can't hear and she can't talk, but she's more woman than all of those who can.' Arch turned Carrie's face with one finger. 'Don't worry, Carrie, I'll get you out of this,' he said. As he spoke, the girl focused on his lips, then nodded vigorously, a wide smile on her lovely face.

'OK, Arch. Here's the deal. You weren't in on the robbery at Vulture City, though I wager you hid the gold. You promise to take Carrie into Wickenburg and I won't press charges against you. Marshal Meade is there, and you tell him I sent you with her. Now. Let her go back to her family. Go to see her as a beau ought to. Court her. Then if she wants to follow you through hell, get her old man's OK on it. And make it legal. If you quit the outlaw trail before you get started, you've got a chance to stay alive long enough to give her a good home and a fine family.

'Laura,' Havelock continued, 'I'd be obliged if you would go into Wickenburg with Arch and Carrie. I'm going to send Horn Stalker too, and you could sort of take care of him.'

'Certainly, Garet,' she said. She stepped around the fire to stand between the couple and the wounded Indian.

'What about me?'

Havelock skewered Donovan with his eyes. 'Yeah, Captain Donovan. What about you? Ride to Wickenburg and M.K. Meade will have you in chains. Stay here and the Apaches will make you wish you had never left my jail. It's your choice, but if I were you, I'd forget about the Vulture gold and strike out for parts unknown. There may be someplace on the outlaw trail fit for you. Brown's Hole. Round Valley. Hole in the Wall. But the hideaways are getting fewer and fewer. Before long, there won't be any more.'

'What gives you the idea that we can just ride out of here?'

'Chief Puma gave his word,' Havelock said.

Disbelief filled Donovan's face.

'I killed Puma's grandson during the firefight Laura started,' Havelock said. 'He wants me bad enough to let you go free if I surrender.'

'Garet! No!' Laura turned on her brothers. 'You two may be willing to just ride out of here while Marshal Havelock turns himself over to those heathens, but I'm not. I will fight. If we win, fine. If not, we save our last bullets for ourselves.' With her mouth set in a firm line of resolve. Laura jacked open her Winchester, checked the mechanism, snapped the action shut, wiped off the ejected shell, and pushed it into the rifle's magazine.

'They won't kill me, Laura,' Havelock said.

She stopped, a question in her eyes.

'They are going to let me run. I get a head start and the warriors try to catch me. If I get away, I go free. If not, I'm dead. Thank you for the thought but I gave my word.'

Laura nodded. The tears on her cheeks glinted in the firelight.

'How many horses have you got?' asked Havelock.

'Six. And two pack-mules,' Arch Donovan said.

'Give Donovan two. He can go wherever he wants. The rest of you ride straight to Wickenburg. You can make town by late tomorrow if you start around midnight.' Havelock paused, then asked: 'How's your water?'

Again Arch Donovan answered. 'There's a spring way back in the cave. Not a heavy flow, but enough to fill the canteens and water the horses before we leave.'

'Good.' Havelock hunkered down beside the wounded Yavapai. The old Indian lay on his right side, his head cushioned on the crook of his arm. Havelock put a hand to Horn Stalker's forehead. 'Can you ride, my brother?'

'I will do what I must, Iron Knee, as will you. The run against death is not pleasant. You may wish to die many times before it is over. Be sly as the coyote, my friend. And remember. He who runs swiftest does not always win. Apaches are a proud people. Sometimes pride blinds them. Remember the bighorn. The Apache hunt him. But often, he escapes the Apache arrow. You may too.'

Havelock held out his hand, palm up. Horn Stalker clasped it wrist-to-palm in the way of the Yavapai. Havelock stood and turned back to the fire.

'Now. If you can spare me a chunk of that meat and a spot of that coffee . . . '

Laura cut a large piece of meat and handed it to Havelock, knife and all. Then she poured a cup full of scalding coffee.

Havelock sat on a boulder near the wall of the cave and attacked the meat. The taste of fire-roasted antelope brought bursts of saliva into his mouth, and as the meat filled his stomach, he felt his tired muscles reviving. *I'll sleep until the middle of the night*, he thought, *then eat a little more. Chances are I won't get the opportunity to sleep at the Apache camp*.

'Laura,' he said, automatically turning to her. 'I'm going to catch a few winks. Would you wake me when you're ready to leave?'

131

'Surely, Garet.'

She'd used his first name again, and he liked the sound of it. He wondered if a woman like Laura would ever consider ... nah, not a half-breed Cherokee.

His dreams put him back in Oklahoma again, tied to a cottonwood with a Yankee captain in red knee-high boots taking aim at his left knee. He heard the voice again and again, over and over, mocking him. *I'm Donovan. Barnabas Donovan. Buzz to my friends.* Again he felt himself cringing as black powder propelled the pistol ball into his knee.

Havelock muttered and groaned as he slept. His tossing brought Laura to his side. She put a hand to his forehead. No fever, but the moisture there felt oily. She got a tin of water and a scrap of cloth and began bathing Havelock's face and neck. The cooling effect quieted him and he slept, with a frown of concentration on his dark face.

7

Havelock woke before the others left for Wickenburg. Slowly he surveyed the cave. Three forms lay in blankets around the feeble fire. The light but steady flow of the spring cooled the cave. The breath of air moving past told Havelock of another opening in the back. Whether big enough for a man to get through, he had no way of knowing. Laura turned over.

'I see you are awake,' she said. 'I was just going to rouse you.'

'Thanks. I feel better.' Havelock rubbed a hand across his face. Though he wore a moustache, he didn't like a stubble.

'Would you have shaving gear?' he asked Laura.

'Arch does. I'll get it for you.'

Laura rose and moved back into the darkness. She wore men's clothing again, ready for the ride to Wickenburg. Havelock placed a few sticks of wood on the dying fire. It smoked angrily for a few moments, but by the time Laura returned, flames greedily devoured the wood. A tin can of water sat next to the fire, heating.

'Buzz left,' she said as she handed him a razor, strop, a bit of soap, and a trade mirror.

Havelock was silent for a time.

'Where did he go?' he asked.

'Knowing my older half-brother,' she said, emphasizing the *half*, 'he'll want to get out of Apache territory quickly. I'd guess Ehrenburg.'

'What about the gold?'

'Arch told him. I think you talked my little brother off the outlaw trail. Perhaps he really is in love with Carrie.'

'If he's gonna do the right thing, he should turn the gold over to Marshal Meade.'

'He says he just packed it around. Says it was Buzz's operation, start to finish.'

Havelock chewed on the end of a thin stick. Then he threw it into the fire and turned on his heel.

'OK. But take my word. Things'll end up different. Different from what Donovan wants. Different from what he figures. I'll see to it, so help me God.'

Laura didn't move. Havelock's fierce words brought tears to her eyes, and he felt them on him as he walked toward the rear of the cave.

The horses snorted at Havelock. He spoke to them softly, and set about preparing them for the run to Wickenburg. He kept busy, working to help keep his mind off the dawn, off his coming run. Then, on the spur of the moment, he took a few things from his saddlebag, wrapped them in a spare shirt, and stood on tiptoe to push the bundle onto an outcropping ledge. The air coming in through the cavern's mouth brought the smell of woodsmoke from the fire.

'Marshal Havelock?' Arch Donovan spoke from a few yards away.

'I'm here.'

The young man felt his way to where Havelock saddled a tall bay mare. 'I'm some kind of fool,' he said.

'How's that?'

'Well, I started out figuring to get rich and buy me a spread somewheres. Picking up the governor's daughter was insurance, just in case. But I never thought I'd snatch a girl like Carrie. Why, she trusts me. Not many grown folks would do that. And right now I kinda feel like any spread I got wouldn't be quite right without her.'

'You'll have to wait a while. She's not quite of age.'

'I can do that.'

'She'll be some pack for you to carry. You'd have to be ears and mouth for the both of you.'

'I know that.'

They worked in silence, neither wanting to say more. Soon the canteens were full, the gear stowed, and the horses watered. Havelock led the first horse toward the cave opening.

'Being needed's not a bad feeling, Marshal. I don't think I'll mind being ears and mouth for her.' Arch spoke softly, but the sound of his determination rang loud. Havelock had never felt that way. Trusted, yes; feared, yes; needed, no. In a way, he envied the young man. He wondered if half-breeds really were different.

The odor of strong coffee greeted Havelock in the main part of the cave. He handed the reins of the horse to Laura and reached for the steaming cup she held out.

Horn Stalker was up, sitting crosslegged by the fire. His face was still flushed, but he seemed to have more strength. He sniffed at the breeze coming in the mouth of the cave.

'I smell wetness on the wind,' he said. 'There will be rain before the sun sets.'

'That means a fifty-fifty chance,' Havelock said, 'but I hope you're right.'

The Yavapai did not reply. He merely looked long and deep into Havelock's black eyes. Then he smiled.

'Here. Take some of this singed meat. It will give you strength. A man cannot run well with only coffee in his belly.'

Havelock gnawed at the meat Horn Stalker gave him. Laura dumped a handful of sliced bacon into a skillet and soon the smell of sizzling food filled the cave. Biscuits baked in a covered dutch oven by the side of the fire.

Before the others left, Havelock ate the good part of a pound of bacon, two large chunks of broiled antelope, and half a dozen hot biscuits dipped in bacon fat. He had one thing to do before returning to the Apaches. Havelock got a can of tallow from his saddlebags. Back at the fire, he rolled the left leg of his pants up to expose the brace and ruination of his knee. He heard Laura's gasp as she saw the exploded scar where his kneecap had been.

He removed the brace of leather and iron, hinged in the center to work with his leg, shafted on each side and wrapped tightly about the leg with six-inch leather bands and a system of laces and buckles.

'Have to grease this thing now and again or it squeaks,' Havelock said. 'I can't walk far without it, and I certainly need it to run.' He dipped his finger into the tallow and began working the grease into the leather on the outside, along the iron shafts, and into the hinges.

'Garet. You can't run with that knee!' Laura's voice was tight with concern. 'Come with us. We can be half-way to Wickenburg before the Apaches know you've left.'

'No, Laura. I will run. I've been in tight spots before. As Horn Stalker said, the man who runs swiftest does not always win the race. With a little luck I'll be able to come calling on you . . . except I don't know if you cotton to half-breeds or where to find you. Where would I look, anyway?'

Laura colored slightly. 'I'll stay at the hotel in Wickenburg until I hear what's happened to you.'

'Fine. That's where I'll look first.' Havelock smiled.

'Garet?' The name was almost a whisper.

Havelock continued strapping the brace back in place. He didn't look up.

Laura knelt beside him and put her cool fingers on the scar of his knee. 'Was it an accident?'

'No, Laura. It was war. I was tied to a tree. A Yankee captain very carefully shot me in that knee. His powder must have been a bit wet because the ball only shattered the kneecap without damaging the joint.'

'Did you ever find out who it was?'

'He told me. He said his name was Donovan. Barnabas Donovan. And that his friends called him Buzz.'

Laura stood up, her face white, one hand to her lips. Tears streaked her cheeks but she made no sound. Havelock finished fastening the brace. As he stood up, she said: 'I'm sorry, Garet. So sorry.'

Havelock said nothing.

Horn Stalker was mounted, hunched over his pony's withers. Arch Donovan helped Carrie into the saddle and made ready to swing up himself. Havelock took the sobbing woman by the elbow and guided her to the offside of his lineback dun.

'Don't worry about me,' he said. 'You have your work cut out getting this bunch to Wickenburg. Chin up. I'm counting on you.'

Though her eyes were full of tears, Laura smiled. She mounted and sat straight in the saddle.

'We'll make it, Garet, so help me.' She kicked the horse forward, and the group followed: four dark forms in their saddles, the last leading the two pack-mules.

Within minutes the hoofbeats faded into the night.

Havelock banked the fire and walked down the slope toward the Apache camp. With the dawn, he would run for his life.

Less than a quarter-mile from the cave, two Apaches appeared behind

Havelock. They kept their distance, watchful, apparently satisfied to wait for the run.

The old chief sat at the fire when Havelock arrived. He motioned the marshal over.

'Sit, Iron Knee. We talk.'

'Yes, Father,' Havelock said, with respect.

'Do you know the run?'

'I have heard.'

'I tell you.' The old man peered at Havelock. 'You start first. After a time, my warriors run after you. At dawn, I decide how far you start. It is justice to do so. You will run as your mother bore you. With only a cover for your loins. And your iron knee.'

'Tell me, Father. Can a man run faster than death?'

A smile touched the old chief's lips.

'Yes,' he said. 'It has been done.'

Havelock rolled a smoke and offered it to Puma. The chief took it, lit it deftly with a burning twig, and inhaled deeply.

'The white man's tabac is good,' he said.

Havelock held out the bag of Bull Durham and pack of papers. He didn't smoke himself, except on formal occasions with the Indians, but he always carried tobacco and could shape cigarettes as well as any waddie.

The old man accepted Havelock's gift. 'Too bad fate made you kill my grandson,' he said.

'I did what I did.'

'Run well, Iron Knee. I sleep.' Puma, standing straight in defiance of his countless years, turned away from Havelock and ducked into a brush wickiup.

The fire burned low, becoming a handful of glowing coals. Still Havelock sat, motionless as a stone. Just before dawn cracked the sky, Tom Morgan squatted at Havelock's side.

'How's the knee?' Morgan asked.

'Good as can be expected. It'll hold up as long as I do.'

'Here, this might help.' Morgan held

out five pellets about the size of peas.

'What's that?'

'I don't rightly know. The Pueblos make them from a desert plant. They kill pain, Havelock. Believe me. You'll be glad for them. I would never have made it through this,' Morgan held up the stump of his right arm, 'if it hadn't been for these.'

Havelock accepted the pellets.

'Can I offer a bit of advice?' Morgan asked.

'Any time, Tom. You know that.'

The black man picked up a stick with his left hand and drew awkwardly in the dust by the fire.

'Eagle Eye Mountain is here,' he said, drawing a circle. 'The Wickenburg-Ehrenburg stage road runs on the far side. The road's about twenty-five miles off. I don't think you'd better try for it.'

Morgan drew a line due east from Eagle Eye. 'Here's Nigger's Well, dug by a friend of mine about ten years ago. He was gonna set up a way station, but the Apaches got him first. Not many people know the well. You could water up there before hitting out for Wickenburg.'

'I'll give it some thought,' said Havelock, not telling Morgan he'd decided to run westward.

A line of fire touched the eastern sky. Feathers of clouds turned coral pink in the west. And far to the south, over the Sea of Cortez, a warm wet wind blew northward and thunderheads formed, piling up until they had clawed their way almost seven miles above the level of the sea.

The storm front moved across the desert, over the Gila Mountains, and on toward the Big Horns with surprising speed. In the Big Horn Mountains, sheep and bears and desert cougars sought shelter.

The sun peeked over the rim of the world, and three strong warriors seized Havelock. He clenched his hands, but did not struggle. In moments they had stripped him and fitted him with a leather loincloth. His feet and head were bare; his brace was dark against his leg. After they finished, he shoved one of the green pellets into his mouth. The other four went into a fold in the waistband of the loincloth. He'd surely need the pain deadened if he were to run barefoot in the desert.

Puma came from his wickiup. He waved fragrant smoke from special herbs up and down Havelock's body.

'Iron Knee, slayer of my grandson, you run. The Great Spirit will decide if you live or die.'

'Yes, Father,' Havelock said.

The fourteen warriors Puma had chosen for Havelock's trial gathered in the clearing. They stared at Havelock, focusing on their prey. They held knives and war axes as bows and arrows were not allowed during the run of death.

'Look,' said Puma. 'See the stone with the white face.' The small boulder protruded from the desert about fifty paces away.

'I see it,' Havelock said.

'When you reach that stone, Iron

Knee, my warriors come. Go.'

Havelock walked toward the stone, trying not to cringe. He stepped with care to minimize damage to his feet. His bare soles had to carry him far if he were to outrun Puma's braves.

Just before reaching the stone, Havelock stopped and threw a panic-stricken look over his shoulder. The warriors screamed, and shook their weapons.

He set out at a ground-eating trot. He often ran in the desert outside Vulture City, to exercise his knee as much as to build stamina. He knew he could keep this pace for hours, except the desert floor ate into the soles of his bare feet.

Havelock passed the stone. With a roar, the warriors sprinted after him. Again, he glanced over his shoulder. A lean warrior ran a dozen strides ahead of the pack. Havelock broke into a sprint, angling to the left. The lead warrior came whooping after him, waving a war axe.

A gully sliced the flank of Eagle Eye Mountain less than a quarter of a mile away. The lead warrior now loped nearly fifty yards ahead of the pack.

Havelock demanded more speed of his tender feet. He plunged over the lip of the gully and out of sight. He dove sharply to the left, and moved uphill. Moments later he found a large sandstone shelf cropping up in the bottom of the wash. He hid behind it with a shard of shale in his hand, forcing himself to breathe slowly and deeply.

The lead warrior scrambled over the edge of the gully. He let out a screech when he saw Havelock's bloody footprints leading up the gully, and dashed in pursuit.

Havelock lay in wait, but the warrior nearly escaped. The naked marshal leaped from behind the sandstone shelf and collided with the speeding brave, knocking him down, but almost failed to get an arm around the neck and under his chin. The brave writhed, but Havelock's arms and shoulders held uncommon strength. The hammerlock closed the carotid arteries and blocked the flow of blood to the Apache's brain. His body went limp. Havelock snatched up the brave's axe. Shouts from other pursuers said he had no time to take the moccasins. He plunged up the gully. His first goal — the cave — was only moments away.

The shouts of the warriors drew nearer. Havelock had little time. Thanks to the Pueblo drug, however, pain did not incapacitate him. He ran on, jumping from rock to rock as the gully got steeper. Then he dashed for the cavern. He moved quickly yet carefully. The thin soles of his feet still had to carry him a long way.

As he topped the gully's bank, warriors boiled around a bend and caught sight of him. They screamed and spread out, some launching themselves at the walls of the gully, hoping to outflank him. But he was again out of sight by the time they reached the top of the gully. Havelock ran for the cave, ignoring the tearing sensations from the soles of his feet.

★   ★   ★

The sun climbed higher in the pale sky. And to the south, thunder rumbled as the storm front pushed into the desert north of the Gila River. Grimly, Havelock stayed ahead of his pursuers. He could not avoid the sharp edges of sandstone, shale, and dried desert wood. They cut. He bled. But he would not give up.

The thunderheads crept closer. A southerly wind came up. The creatures of the desert sought refuge. Soon thirteen Apache warriors clamoring after a naked white man with a leather-and-steel brace on his left leg were all that moved beneath the clouds. The warriors paid no attention to the weather.

Havelock's breath came in great heaves as he topped the rise that fronted the cave. He dashed into the cave, and ran to where the horses had been tied. He retrieved the bundle from the ledge — a shirt, a pair of moccasins, and a knife. He slipped the moccasins on and strode back to the banked fire where the can of tallow lay by the wall of the cave. He quickly smeared all the tallow into the folds of the shirt and wrapped it tightly around the head of the war axe. He shoved the bundled axe head into the banked coals as he listened for Apache pursuit. As the cloth of the shirt caught fire, he heard the warriors scrabbling up the embankment. He ran toward the back of the cavern, shielding the makeshift torch with his body.

The flames melted the tallow, fed on the grease, and lit the way. Smoke from the torch moved ahead of Havelock, leading toward the opening at the other end.

Knife in hand he paused. He heard nothing. Perhaps the braves were cautious about plunging into a dark cavern.

Beyond the spring, the cave narrowed until Havelock had to turn sideways to edge along. Light from his torch showed sand on the floor of the cave, and in the sand, the five-pad footprints of another kind of puma — the desert cougar from which the old chief took his name. Havelock could only push on.

Suddenly, a dark void — the torch burned, but its light no longer reflected from stone walls. Cautiously, Havelock moved into a large chamber.

The cavern had probably been carved by the waters that were now a tiny spring. Dimly, Havelock saw stalactites and stalagmites at the far side of the chamber, but a tumble of jagged rocks cascaded down the near side. The thin roof of the cavern had caved in like a badly shored mine shaft. High up the slope of tumbled rock, Havelock saw a sliver of daylight. His way out.

Shoving the knife into his leather loincloth and holding the torch high, Havelock started up. Ten feet, twenty. Then from across the chamber came the soft warning cough of the cougar. Havelock froze.

The big cats rarely attacked unless provoked, and they didn't like fire. Havelock hoped his torch was enough. The cougar's eyes reflected the light of the torch from the other side of the chamber. Then the eyes disappeared.

The cat jumped from its ledge and padded out of the chamber the way Havelock came in.

Havelock waited.

After a while he continued his climb. At the top, he threw the sputtering torch back into the cavern and pulled out the knife. The opening was large enough, but a piñon pine had taken root by a large boulder above the hole and its branches formed a thick cover over the exit. Havelock would have to worm his way through the piñon needles while watching out for Apaches. Wind whipped the branches into a frenzy.

Slowly Havelock poked his head through the opening. Wind tore at his hair. What once had been a sinkhole now looked like a natural indent, the northern edge a continuation of Eagle Eye Mountain and the southern edge a lip, far above and behind the entrance to the cave.

Havelock grasped a piñon branch and pulled himself into the thicket. He bellied out from under the tree's clutches, took shelter behind the boulder, then surveyed the edges of the indent. No sign of Apaches.

Havelock stood and walked west, keeping to his original plan. As he topped the edge of the indent, a shout from below said he'd been spotted.

At that moment, angry storm clouds blotted the sun, catching the warriors unaware. Lightning preceded the storm which had already filled Centennial Wash and flooded the Gila River.

Intent on their prey, the Apaches had failed to notice the strength of the approaching storm. But they halted as one when a mighty bolt ripped a gnarled old juniper and left it smoking on the side of the mountain. Few things frightened Apache warriors; one was lightning.

Havelock climbed for the ridge that marked the Big Horn divide. The moccasins helped but as the effect of the pellet wore off, pain from the damaged soles of his feet shot up his legs. His head throbbed from Laura's bullet, and his knee could not put up with much more strain.

Another bolt of lightning struck. Closer. The Apaches darted about in jerky circles shouting, *Pis! Pis!*, in imitation of Pise, the speckled night-hawk, who could dodge lightning bolts.

Havelock topped the divide as the heavy curtain of rain hit. He concentrated so totally on climbing the steep slope that he was unprepared for the drop off on the other side. The rain smashed him down the sharp incline. He struggled for balance. His leather moccasins slipped on the wet rock. He plunged downward, rolled like a log by the runoff.

The rain drove the dancing Apaches to shelter and turned the desert into a sea of mud. Every gully and wash foamed with floodwaters that carried the dead bodies of animals, branches torn from living trees, and whatever flotsam lay in the way.

Havelock continued downhill with the gathering force of water. He smashed a shoulder against the rocks and lost his knife. His scream was lost in the roar of falling water. Half-way to the bottom, he snagged up against an old juniper deadfall, banging his injured head on its solid trunk.

⋆　⋆　⋆

Guttural Apache voices woke Havelock. His head felt as though Laura had used it for a target again, but he heard the warriors say his name, Iron Knee. Then someone must have mentioned lightning because several braves shouted 'Pis! Pis!'

Havelock could hear the Indians but

not see them. The run-off had washed him far under the deadfall and then piled on sticks, branches, leaves, pack-rats' nests, and other debris.

He lay on his right side, facing the juniper's trunk. The footsteps and voices of the Apaches receded up the slope. He didn't open his eyes for a long time. Perhaps he slept. Or maybe he lost consciousness.

Thunder rumbled and rain fell further north as the storm moved onto the Colorado Plateau. At the Apache rancheria, Puma listened as his braves told how Iron Knee had run to the cave. How a mountain lion had come out afterward, bounding up the mountain away from them. How the death runner had suddenly appeared high up the mountainside, near the divide. How the lightning had come when they tried to pursue him. And how he disappeared as the rain passed. Perhaps, they ventured, he had become a mountain cat.

A tiny smile came to the old chief's

face. His totem had protected Iron Knee. And Tom Morgan, lying in a nearby wickiup, heard Puma say:

'The Great Spirit has spoken. My grandson is avenged. His ghost cries no longer for the blood of Iron Knee.'

8

Havelock strained to open his eyes. The slight movement brought blinding pain. Smashing his head against the juniper's trunk had aggravated the effect of Laura's bullet. He couldn't help but groan. Stubs of broken juniper branches had scraped and poked him as the flood shoved him into the deadfall. He'd bled in a dozen places, and one sharp splinter had driven itself deep into the fleshy part of his forearm. He had to extract it, but first he needed to get out of the deadfall.

Stick by stick, sodden leaf by sodden leaf, Havelock removed the flotsam. He held his left arm still, trying not to hit the sliver on anything. At last, when he dragged himself into the open, little daylight remained.

The rainstorm had left water in hollowed-out rocks in the bottom of the wash. Havelock didn't risk standing up.

Just getting out of the deadfall had made him dizzy. The juniper sliver throbbed in his left forearm. Crawling to a rock basin, he sucked at the rainwater. It tasted of mud. It tasted wonderful.

The sun dropped behind the mountains beyond the Colorado River, filling the sky with gold. Although the days were hell-fire hot, temperatures dropped at night. Havelock had only a loincloth for warmth, but he slept.

Havelock's eyes opened with the dawn. His body shook. The edges of the wound where the sliver protruded showed an angry red. Havelock struggled to his feet. He shoved a finger into his breechclout, searching for the painkiller pellets he'd put there. They had melted into a lump. Havelock scooped the goo onto his index finger. He put half in his mouth and left half on a flat sandstone, then bellied down to a rock basin for another drink.

Soon Havelock felt no pain, but he had to cut the splinter out. He struggled to the crest of the ridge, then started back down, retracing his tumble and searching for his knife. The sun was high when he found the knife wedged deep into a crack. Pain racked his battered body, but there were things to do before he could take the last of the painkiller and cut the splinter out.

First he needed fire. He found a piece of flint and used the knife as steel. Strong sparks danced when he struck the flint against the blade. Tinder he got from a rotten log. Broken open, the log supplied a powder that held a spark well. Tiny dry sticks, leaves, and larger chunks of wood completed his preparations. With patience learned from his Cherokee grandfather, he struck spark after spark until one caught in the punky rot and he could coax it into flame.

Havelock kept the fire small, but the sight of it lifted his spirits. He swallowed the rest of the painkiller and again sucked water from a rock basin.

For poultice, Havelock sliced ears

from a nearby prickly pear, seared their spines off over the fire, then beat them to a pulp with the handle of the knife. The fleshy scent of cactus smelled fresh and clean. From a nearby juniper he cut long strips of inner bark to use as string, then sharpened the knife with a sandstone and stropped it on one of his moccasins. He had to cut the splinter out while the painkiller held.

Havelock made a quick deep cut, running the knife point along the splinter. Blood flowed. He grasped the splinter and worked it slowly backwards until it came loose. Blood filled the hole and flowed down his forearm. A handful of prickly pear mush on the wound, covered by an ear with the skin scraped off one side and wrapped with strings of juniper bark completed the dressing.

Prickly-pear fruit, plump, red, and roasted over the fire, took the edge off his hunger. After a long drink of water from the natural tank, Havelock burrowed under an overhanging mesquite to sleep. He'd travel at night.

In Prescott, the governor received a telegram from M.K. Meade. His daughter was safe. And in Wickenburg, four weary travelers slept after their grueling ride. A lone rider leading a spare horse paused under the window of the hotel. He rolled a smoke and struck a lucifer. For an instant, the match lit the face of Barnabas Donovan.

★ ★ ★

By the morning of the second day, Havelock knew he had to move. The wound in his arm was angry but not festering. The rock basins now held little water, and nearby prickly-pear plants were stripped of ripe fruit. His bare skin had toughened with the exposure, but direct sunlight would still burn him.

He bellied down to the dregs in the sandstone basin, drinking all he could hold. His body must store the moisture as he had no canteen or water-bag. With luck, he'd make the stage road before dying of dehydration or sunstroke.

With Eagle Eye Mountain to his right, the battered marshal set out for the stage road, more than twenty miles north. He wore moccasins. The prickly-pear poultice on his wound was wrapped with cedar bark. The knife stuck in his loincloth. His slow pace kept him from sweating and wasting body water, and he stepped carefully so as not to jar his head.

He moved high above the floor of the desert. The horizon stretched across the distance to where the black outline of stony mountains bisected the dark but starry sky.

The desert's a hard land, thought Havelock. *But it's beautiful. It's a living land that's wild and free, and it makes no compromises for puny men who imagine they're great.* Havelock chuckled. He wondered if he'd ever again see his homestead above the Mogollon

Rim. There, a silver ribbon of water ran through flat grasslands flanked by great malpai volcanic stone. Havelock had found the place five years before, when visiting Colonel Corydon Cooley's big white house in the foothills of the White Mountains. He'd filed claim on a half-section and had a man proving up on it. He planned to raise whiteface cattle and good horses on that place . . . someday.

Havelock's mind wandered as he stumbled through the desert night. The dry wind sucked moisture from his body faster than he'd counted on. He'd planned to make ten, maybe twelve, miles during the night, then hole up for the day, and walk the rest of the way the next night.

Then he fell. Stepped right off the edge of a shallow gully and rolled nearly a dozen feet down the side to fetch up against a sandstone ledge. For a moment he lay dazed. *I'm gonna have to quit banging my head against things*, he thought. The fall had torn the cactus poultice from his arm. Blood oozed.

Fortunately, the knife at Havelock's waist had not driven into his groin. He made it to his feet on the third try. He peered through the darkness at the hole in his arm. The bleeding had stopped, but the wound throbbed, an echo of the throbbing in his head.

He tried to climb the side of the gully but didn't have the strength. He went to all fours. Head hanging, he considered the situation. Damn. Maybe Donovan was right. Maybe he was just a 'breed, neither here nor there, nothing anyone would ever want. Laura's image crept across his eyelids. He shook his head. Damn. Get on with it. 'You will not give up!' he shouted. Echoes from the mountain returned his words.

Havelock decided to follow the gully westward to the desert floor. Stumbling onward, he came across a stand of Osage orange and cut a staff from the tough tree to lean on as he plodded on.

The thin soles of his moccasins wore through, and the desert punished his bare feet through gaping holes in the leather. Havelock concentrated on moving forward, avoiding the dim forms of cacti in the dark. The moon rose, bathing the desert in soft blue light, and Havelock made better progress. He'd trudged almost ten miles when the dawn sent fingers of gold into the sky above Eagle Eye Mountain.

Havelock dozed in the shade of a jutting monolith, moving back into the shadow whenever the sun hit him. By evening his arm and head felt better. His feet did not.

Once more, prickly pear provided his food. Without fire, he had to peel the outer skins and spines off with his knife. The fruit gave him moisture and renewed a measure of his strength. With the glory of the sunset, he started out again, still moving north.

Soon his moccasins had no soles, and sticks and stones lacerated his feet. Progress slowed. Without something to cover his feet, he'd never make the stage road. Havelock paused. His head and arm ached dully; his feet hurt as if slashed with razors. He leaned on his staff. No cedar bark here. Cactus wouldn't work. If only he had pain-killer. He stuffed a forefinger into the waistband of his loincloth, searching for a trace of medicine.

Leather loincloth! A long strip of soft doehide about a foot wide, tied at the waist with a thong, with flaps hanging front and back. Covering for his feet — a wide smile cracked Havelock's lower lip.

He cut foot-shaped patches from the loincloth's flaps. Then he sawed a strip away from each side, but left it attached at the back. He punched holes along the sides. Placing a foot on one patch, he grasped the two strips and pulled them across his instep. Back and forth he laced the strips until the patch on his foot resembled a Roman sandal.

With the improvised sandals, he moved much faster, but the stage road remained a good three miles away when the sun topped the divide.

Movement in daylight would sap his strength fast, but the road was so close. He'd promised to go to Wickenburg. He'd promised to bring in Donovan. He'd promised to get back the gold. To many, the promises of a half-breed were worthless; to Havelock, they were priceless.

Havelock focused on the stage road. The hot sun sucked at his pores and scorched his body. A dry wind sprang up, cracked his lips and blotted moisture from his body. He struggled on.

The Ehrenburg-bound stage raised a roostertail of dust as it barreled along the rutted stage road. Havelock didn't notice the Concord until it was almost abreast of him, a mile away. He broke into a shambling run, and hoped the driver or the shotgun rider would see him.

The stage rumbled by. Its dust settled. Havelock staggered into the rutted road, stumbled, and sprawled face down. He lay panting, his breath raising tiny spurts of dust. The stage was gone. It was no use. And he was so tired.

So very tired.

★   ★   ★

Santa Fe Sims drowned an errant stinkbug with a stream of tobacco juice. He rarely missed, with tobacco-induced saliva or with the eighteen-foot bull-whip that hung in a coil from his left shoulder. He could snap a fly from the ear of any horse in the team without touching a hair.

Some thought Santa Fe colorful, with his long white hair, buckskins, walrus moustache and greasy slouch hat, its brim pinned up against the crown with the crossed sabers of the Confederate cavalry. But Wells Fargo hired Santa Fe Sims because he was the best man on the ribbons west of St Louis. Before the war, he drove Murphy freight wagons down the trail to Santa Fe. Under Southern arms, he kept supplies flowing to Lee right up to Appomattox.

When the fighting was over, Santa Fe Sims went back to the trail from which he took his name — who'd want to own up to a first name like Bartholomew anyway — and started cracking whips and singeing mules' ears with epithets.

'Stage leaving,' Santa Fe shouted.

'Should be a smooth run,' said Haycock, the Ehrenburg Wells Fargo agent. 'One sack of mail and two passengers. That can't be worth enough for robbers.'

'A man cain't be too careful. Wouldn't want to get bullet holes in this here brand-spanking-new Concord.' Santa Fe was nonchalant, but proud of his new coach. He clambered up on the box and gathered up the reins.

'Barny,' he called to a youth whose guileless face belied his age and his skill with a shotgun. 'Get them *laydees* and *gennulmun* into the coach. We got a ways to go afore sunset.'

The youth shooed the passengers, a drummer and a portly woman with a kindly face, into the Concord.

'OK, Santa Fe,' Barny said as he climbed up to the box, 'Let 'er rip.'

The whip crack sounded like a rifle shot. The popper at the end came up short of the ear of the offside lead mare by no more than a fine hair. The two spans of horses went from a standstill to a flat-out run in three strides. Santa Fe always liked a dramatic exit.

Out of Ehrenburg, the old Jehu pulled the four-horse team back to a ground-eating gallop. Six hours and two way stations from now he'd pull into Wickenburg, with flair.

Santa Fe was on his second team when young Barny Ellsworth put a hand on his arm. The shotgun rider pointed at a prone figure in the road ahead.

'Looks like a dead Injun,' he shouted.

'You keep your eyes peeled for owlhoots,' Santa Fe said, 'I'll have Sally Mae look that gent over.' The team stopped not ten feet from the naked figure sprawled in the dust.

'Sally Mae.'

'What do you want, Santa Fe?'

'There's an *hombre* in the road ahead what looks either dead or pert near so. Hate to ask a lady, but would you do me a favor and take a look-see?' Santa Fe spat off the downwind side of the Concord.

Sally Mae Peebles opened the Concord's door.

'You know I'm no lady, Santa Fe Sims, and I can take care of myself well enough to examine any man's body, in the road or elsewhere.'

'We just don't want this to be some kind of bushwhacking job, Sally Mae. I know you can care for yourself, which is more than I can say for that drummer man in there, which is why I ast you to have a look-see. Me and Barny will stay up here where we can see.' Santa Fe punctuated his request by jacking a shell into the chamber of his Winchester.

The portly woman stepped down from the stagecoach with a big Dragoon Colt pistol in her capable right hand, hammer cocked. She marched into the road and bent over the prostrate form.

'Santa Fe, this man's badly hurt. Looks like he ran all the way from Phoenix on his bare feet. Got some kind of contraption on his leg, too. Get yourself down here with some water.' Sally Mae put her pistol in its specially made skirt pocket and turned the man over. Santa Fe arrived with a canteen.

'That's Garet Havelock, marshal over to Vulture City,' he said. 'Looks like he's been handled a bit rough.' The tough old Jehu lifted Havelock's head with gentle hands. He tipped the canteen and poured a few drops of water into the slack mouth. At first the water just trickled down the dusty chin. Then Havelock's throat contracted and a tiny bit of muddy Colorado River water slid down his throat. Desperate, Havelock knocked away Sally Mae's arm. He grabbed for the canteen, but Santa Fe held him back.

'Easy now, Havelock. You come some way. You just settle back and let Sally

Mae here take care of you 'til we get to town.'

'Meade,' Havelock croaked. 'Gotta get to Wickenburg. Gotta see Meade.'

'All righty. We'll getcha there. Jest you take 'er easy.'

The stage was back on the road in minutes, heading through the gap toward Wickenburg. The Harcuvar Mountains towered more than 5,000 feet on the left, the Harquahalas soared almost 6,000 on the right.

9

The delay put the stage into Wickenburg just after dark. The rocking Concord released Havelock from fear and anxiety, and he slept so soundly he was unaware when Santa Fe and Barny Ellsworth carried him to a room on the second floor of the hotel. There he sprawled on clean sheets while Laura Donovan salved his cuts and scratches and sunburned skin. Wickenburg had no doctor.

Across the street, a big red-headed man bought Santa Fe Sims a drink.

'I always admired a good man with the ribbons,' the big man said. 'I hear you're one of the best.'

'Son, I cut my teeth on rein leather behind a team of mules. I know every rock between Saint Lou and Santy Fe, an' I've hit 'em all.' Santa Fe slurred his words.

'I saw you come in tonight,' said the man. 'Sure was a pretty sight. But I wondered about you carrying a wounded Indian. Isn't that dangerous?'

' 'T'wan't no Injun. 'Twas Marshal Havelock of Vulture City. Oh, he's half-Cherokee, but a man would think he was all white.' Santa Fe twisted his moustache and tossed back the whiskey remaining in his glass. 'Havelock was purty beat up, he was. Bottoms of his feet looked like chopped steak. Had a hole in his arm, too. Don't reckon he'll be too spry for a spell.'

'Nice talking to you, old-timer. Just wanted to say I enjoyed the show.' The big stranger put a finger to the brim of his hat, saluting Santa Fe Sims, and made his way out of the saloon.

The old Jehu's practiced eye noticed the Smith & Wesson in a fancy rig of intricately tooled and carefully oiled leather that didn't seem to match the big man's rough clothes. That rig belonged to a man who used his gun, but it belonged with fancier duds.

Something didn't fit.

The old muleskinner stared after the retreating form for a moment, then shrugged and turned back to the bar.

'Know that feller?' he asked the barkeep.

The barkeeper stopped polishing a glass.

'He's been hanging around for, oh, three, four days,' he said, then breathed on the glass and started polishing again. 'Seems to be a right enough jasper, though. Everyone's been pretty excited about the governor's daughter being brought in by young Donovan. Don't s'pose anyone paid much attention to this feller. Why?'

'Ah, nothing. He just hit me as a bit strange. Fill 'er up, wouldja?'

The 'keep poured Santa Fe two fingers of the house's best.

Outside the saloon, Donovan slid into the shadows of the overhanging roof and stood for a long moment. He didn't want to risk someone recognizing him. True, he'd grown a stubble and slouched to hide his true height, but now, after Vulture City, too many people hereabouts might know him by sight. And Garet Havelock was still alive. He cursed. *Should've killed that 'breed boy when I had him tied to a cottonwood back in the Nations*, he thought, and ground his teeth. *Should've done more than just shoot him in the knee. Always was too sentimental for my own good.*

The desert breeze brought a whiff of sage. Out there, a lot of gold lay buried. Arch had shoveled it under and he'd told his elder brother how to find it. Two men knew, and that was one too many. If Arch hadn't gone pie-eyed over that girl, if he'd not started listening to that 'breed lawman, well, then maybe he could have been trusted. Not now, though. Not now. Donovan smirked and reached for the makings in his vest pocket. He'd silence Arch. He turned to the wall, struck a lucifer, lit his smoke and sucked in a lungful of rank Bull Durham.

The girl had gone back to the governor in Prescott. Sooner or later, Arch would come down for a drink, and die. But before that, Donovan gave himself another job — get rid of the half-breed kid from the Indian Nations.

Donovan kept to the shadows until he was at the back door of the hotel. The door was unlocked, but then, nobody locked doors. He catfooted up the back stairs.

The wall lamp lit up the hallway so Donovan snuffed it out, retreated into the gloom, and settled back to wait.

Moments later, Laura came out of the second room on the left with a pan in her hand. She hurried downstairs without looking around. Donovan scowled. He had found Havelock's room, but he cursed Laura — his own flesh and blood — for siding with the half-breed lawman.

Rage pounded in Donovan's chest, and a red mist came up before his eyes. As he took gigantic steps down the hall, the echo of his pounding boots rang in the narrow confines.

He tested the door with a big fist. It would not open. Even in his anger, Donovan knew he didn't have time to break it down. But every room in the hotel was the same. Angling the Smith & Wesson so the bullets would smash into the bed, Donovan fired five shots in a single roll of sound. Gunsmoke billowed and the hall filled with the acrid odour of burnt black powder.

Immediately he stepped into the adjoining room and strode to the window, ejecting spent shells and reloading the pistol as he walked. He shoved the gun back into its holster, wrenched open the window, climbed out on the ledge, lowered himself until he hung by his fingers, then dropped into the dark alley below.

Donovan casually walked from the alley onto the boardwalk and down the street to the saloon. He pushed his way through the batwings and joined the rowdy bunch bucking the tiger far in the rear.

Just as Donovan joined the revelers

in the saloon, Laura reached the hotel's second-story landing, with the manager a step behind.

'Mr Havelock,' the manager called as they rushed for Havelock's room. 'Mr Havelock!'

Havelock opened the shattered door as they arrived.

'Oh, Garet,' Laura cried. 'Are you all right?'

'I had time to roll off the bed before he shot,' Havelock said. 'Whoever did it would have got me for sure if he'd have sneaked up instead of pounding down the hall making all that racket.

'Sorry, Mr Mendelssohn,' he said to the manager. 'I'm afraid your good feather tick is full of holes.'

'Not to worry, Mr Havelock. Marshal Meade said he'd pay your bills so I reckon he'll be good for the tick as well.' The manager adjusted his glasses and peered at the bullet-wrecked door. 'Have you any idea who did this?'

'I was going to ask you the same

thing.' Havelock drooped as the adrenaline in his system depleted. He put a hand on the wall for support. 'Mind if I sit down?' he asked. 'Got to get off these feet.' He limped to the bed and sat.

Laura had not spoken.

'Miss Donovan saw no one on the way downstairs, did you ma'am?' Mendelssohn said.

Laura's answer came through colorless lips.

'Someone was there and I didn't even notice. The hall lamp was out. The whole end of the hall was dark. Anyone could have been there. But why? Who knows Marshal Havelock is here?'

'Obviously somebody knows I'm here, and wishes I weren't. Permanently.' Havelock hobbled to the commode, poured a glass of water from the porcelain pitcher, and gulped the fluid down. He turned to the manager. 'Now, if you'll get me a weapon, I'll take care of myself.'

The manager scurried out. Havelock sat back down on the edge of the bed.

Feathers from the holes in the tick floated about. He studied the palms of his hands, looking for words. He didn't find any.

Angry shouts came from the saloon. Then a pistol barked. Once. Twice. A horse thundered off into the night. Then a dozen or so more. All was confusion and shouting.

The manager reappeared in the open door, his face full of shock and disbelief. Behind him stood Marshal Meade. The marshal spoke first to Laura.

'I'm sorry, miss. Your brother was just shot down. It doesn't look like he's going to make it. He's asking for you. I know it's not fitting for a lady to go into a saloon, but I figured it was better not to move him. Would you come?'

Laura fled down the stairs. Havelock moved to the window. Moments later, he watched her slim form push through the swinging doors. Moments ago, someone had shot at him through the door of his room. Now a saloon shooting had put Arch down. A strong odor of Buzz Donovan filled Havelock's nostrils — ruthless smell, tinged with blood. He licked his lips. *Wish my damn feet didn't hurt so much*, he thought.

'It was a put-up, Garet,' Meade said. 'That *pistolero* wanted the boy dead. A posse's took off after him. Maybe the boys'll catch up.'

Havelock shook his head. Donovan was his job. His reputation rested on capturing that outlaw. If he didn't do the job, he'd go back to being just another ne'er-do-well half-breed as far as townspeople were concerned.

'They won't catch him,' Havelock said. 'Unless I'm mistaken, they're chasing Buzz Donovan. They'll come back empty-handed. A whole bunch riding around in the desert raising a lot of dust won't get the job done. It'll take one man. And he'll have to go careful.'

'Donovan? Why would he shoot his own brother?' Meade's brow creased.

'Half-brother,' Havelock corrected,

185

automatically. 'Arch hid the Vulture gold. With the boy dead, Donovan figures he'll have that hundred thousand all to himself. One man will have to catch him and bring him in for murder. Or maybe not bring him in.'

In his mind, Havelock searched for Donovan's trail. Five days ago, he'd run from the Apaches. Now, the wound in his arm had scabbed over. The sunburn no longer pained him, and his head had quit throbbing at last. The sleep he'd gotten on the stagecoach had done him good.

Havelock's feet were a different problem. Bits of rock and sand had worked into the cuts on their soles. Laura had dug out most of the debris only a few hours ago. He could stand on his feet, but that was all. He left bloody prints as he returned to bed. His feet thanked him for getting his weight off them again.

But Donovan could not be put off because of sore feet. Havelock knew if he didn't stay on Donovan's trail, the outlaw would get the gold, run out of the state, and sit around on his backside thumbing his nose at the law in Arizona. Havelock had to keep up the pressure, had to let the outlaw know Arizona law was on his trail. Wait, not Arizona law, federal law. Havelock was a deputy US marshal.

'Marshal Meade, I can't go down there to help Laura. I'd be obliged if you would.' As Meade was going out through the door, Havelock added: 'And keep an ear and an eye open for anything that might help us find out what Donovan's up to.' Havelock held up a hand to stop the marshal's retort. 'Yeah, I know that you were law-manning before I was housebroke, I just wanted to jog your memory a little.'

Meade grinned and left, closing the bullet-riddled door behind him. Havelock lay back and swung his legs up onto the bed. A tiny cloud of white feathers flew from the bullet holes in the tick, but they didn't keep him from falling asleep.

When he woke, Laura was there. Her face was a mirror of pain, but there were no tears. She had them locked up inside.

Havelock looked a question at her.

'He's still hanging on. Barely.' The tears threatened to break the lock.

'Did he leave any word for Carrie?'

'He's called her name a lot. He had a riddle for you, too. He even smiled when he said to tell you 'cottonwoods in the afternoon'.'

Havelock turned the words over in his mind, but found no special meaning. From the window, he watched the traffic on the dusty main street of Wickenburg: tall freight wagons with three spans of mules moved south to Vulture City; two itinerant cowboys in shotgun chaps probably headed for Verde Valley; a buckboard driven by a pert black-haired woman, obviously of some means; a gaggle of miners, rough in their canvas trousers and heavy boots, bound for a liquid breakfast at the saloon.

Old Henry Wickenburg — the same man who found and named the Vulture Mine — had chosen a good site for his town. Roads from three major Arizona settlements met there. The rutted track leading south through Vulture City went to Phoenix. The way north went to Prescott, the territorial capital, and to Camp Verde, the largest army post in the area. And the westward stage road struck a line to Ehrenburg, the last stop for the Colorado River steamboats and vital supply center for the territory. Wickenburg bustled.

Laura spoke to Havelock's back.

'Garet, you have never asked me why I shot you out there in the desert.'

He turned. 'I'd be dead if you'd have wanted it that way. I decided not push my luck.'

'Buzz told us, Arch and me, that Vulture City had an Indian for a lawman. He said you used the badge to exact your own revenge on white men, that more than a dozen men had been hanged on that ironwood tree in the

189

plaza. He said in your town there were no trials, only hangings.'

Havelock knew better than to say anything.

'Buzz said I'd have to kill you. That if I didn't, you'd kill us all. He said Indians have no concept of mercy, that you were half-Indian and revenge was all you would think of once you got Carrie back.'

She faced Havelock.

'But you came to help me when the Apaches had me pinned down. And you didn't even know who I was.' A tear worked its way out the corner of her eye and rolled down her cheek. She sniffled.

'I'd have done the same for anyone up against three-to-one odds,' Havelock said. 'I just evened things up somewhat.'

'Buzz is my brother. I felt I had to free him. That's why I shot you. But I couldn't just kill you. Then he wouldn't leave you a gun. Or even a knife. He said the desert would take care of you, save him the trouble. Then he laughed that awful laugh. That's when I realized my brother is more than a thief. He's a killer.'

Once more tears made their silent way down Laura's face. Her voice quavered. 'He shot Arch, his own brother. And Arch may die. Buzz wants the Vulture gold. Arch told him where it's hidden and Buzz made him promise not to tell anyone else. Not even me. And he didn't. Arch always keeps his promises.'

Laura crossed the room and sat beside Havelock on the bed. Slowly she lowered her head to his shoulder. Great sobs shook her body. Havelock awkwardly patted her shoulder as she cried.

★　★　★

The posse dragged back at dawn. The shooter had slipped them in the wilderness near Cave Creek; no telling where he was headed, they said. Havelock figured Donovan's destination was a new gold town called Crown

King. There was no law at Crown King, and that made the town a good place for someone on the run.

'I'd best go after Donovan, Marshal,' Havelock said to M.K. Meade. 'I'll be needing the best horse you can find and grub for three days.'

'Your lineback dun's been resting for four days and eating the federal government out of house and home. Is he good enough?' Meade grinned.

'That dun sure beats walking, and I've done enough walking lately to last me the rest of my life.' Havelock returned the grin.

'Gimme a list of whatever you need,' Meade said. 'I'll make sure you get outta here well prepared.'

Later, Havelock limped from the hotel to the livery stable on tender moccasined feet. Dressed as he was, he looked half-Indian. His breeches were tucked into knee-high Apache moccasins. He wore his new dark-maroon flannel shirt with the shirt-tail out and the bottom button undone so he could easily reach the brand new Colt model 1873 Frontier .44 pistol stuck in his waistband. He pulled the flat-rimmed, flat-crowned plainsman's hat low over his eyes. He could wear the hat straight now, as the furrow left by Laura's bullet was well scabbed over.

Besides the pistol, a .44-40 Winchester saddle gun swung easily in his left hand. A big Bowie knife rode his left hip. A slimmer knife fitted inside the leg of his left moccasin, and a third knife, carefully balanced for throwing, hung down the back of his neck on a leather thong. Once again, he had sewn five loops in the crown of his hat to hold five extra rounds of .44 caliber ammunition. Meade had gotten everything on Havelock's list.

The lineback seemed glad to see Havelock. That horse loved the trail. Born and bred in the desert, he was as good as one of Beal's camels at going without water. Havelock checked the dun's hoofs. Each was covered with iron-hard rawhide.

Havelock inspected the saddlebags — bacon, hardtack, coffee, flour, sugar, a frying-pan, lucifers, and fifty rounds of .44 caliber cartridges that fitted rifle and pistol. A slicker and blankets were rolled tightly and tied behind the cantle. A small coffee-pot hung behind the saddlebags. A big four-quart canteen dangled on one side of the pommel and a sixty-foot rawhide lariat on the other. Havelock fingered the new deputy US Marshal badge Meade had given him. Things were about as ready as they were going to get.

Wincing as his weight went on his tender right foot, Havelock heaved himself into the saddle. He turned the dun's head east down the long main street. Laura stood at the door of the hotel as he rode by, shading her eyes against the glare of the sun. She was still there when Havelock rode over the rise that marked the edge of town, and he could see her in his mind long after that.

At last he shook himself free of her

image. Lawmen trailing outlaws couldn't get the job done by mooning over a woman, he figured. Instead, he turned his mind to Arch's message — cottonwoods in the afternoon. Noodling that message took the better part of the day. Then he turned to Donovan.

Donovan was a gregarious type, no good at being alone. He'd seek company, but avoid the law. That combination had Crown King written all over it. Havelock rode straight for the gold-rush town.

10

Despite its auspicious name, Crown King offered only a collection of canvas tents and rough lumber structures. Two buildings stood out among the hovels: Anderson's saloon and dance hall, and the assay office of the Crowned King mine. The livery was merely a shack and a pole corral.

Havelock left his dun at the livery and walked up the steep main street to Anderson's without a noticeable limp. Two days in the saddle had gone a long way toward healing his feet. He pinned the new deputy US marshal's star Meade had given him out of sight on the backside of his shirt-pocket flap.

Anderson's offered a free lunch and Havelock ate heartily. Then, nursing a beer, he bellied against the bar. The bartender liked to talk. Havelock listened.

'I'll tell you, mister. It's been pure hell around here lately. Ever since Big Phil Jackson and his rowdies showed up.'

'Got everybody pretty well hoorawed, have they?'

'That they do. And for good reason. Four miners have turned up dead. With Big Phil carryin' papers saying they signed their claims over to him before their unfortunate demises.

'Now Big Phil's pushing Miss Sally Mae Peebles to sell her claim.'

Havelock straightened at the name.

'Sally Mae? Would she be a big woman? Fortyish and tough as four-penny nails? Blond hair, what you can see of it, and baby-pink skin?'

'That's Sally Mae all right. Everyone in these parts takes kindly to her. She's usually the one who tends anyone what happens to get hurt ... mining accidents, shootings, knifings, the like. And there being no doctor around here — '

Havelock cut in. 'Where's she at?'

'Her claim's up on the hill to the left, past the Crowned King. She calls it the Consolation. You can't miss it.'

Havelock reached for his Winchester and walked away without another word, leaving the half-full beer-glass on the bar. But he didn't go straight to Sally Mae's claim. He took a good look around first. He saw how Crown King was essentially a huge gully formed by the Hassayampa. Most of the mining claims were in smaller gullies that carried the run-off of the infrequent rains into the main creek. The Crowned King was in the largest of these gullies. The Consolation was in the next offshoot on the opposite side of the creek. Main Street led up the Crowned King side of the creek. Nobody could approach the Consolation except from the front, unless they were half-mountain goat.

After he'd gotten the local geography firmly in mind, Havelock started up the broad, steep path to the Consolation. He was met by the crack of a rifle and a shower of rock chips at his feet.

'One more step and the hole will be in your head, mister.' Sally Mae's voice was mellow, but she meant business.

'Garet Havelock,' he announced, holding his rifle above his head with both hands.

'Walk slow, mister. And keep those hands up there. They make a good rack for that rifle.'

Havelock did as he was told.

Sally Mae recognized him as his face came out of the shadows.

'You should be in bed,' she said. 'What brings you to Crown King?'

'Heard you was having trouble with Big Phil Jackson. I know him, and I've handled his type. Thought I could help.'

'You can. I think he'll be over tonight. You're more than welcome. I only got two men on the place and neither one is much with a gun.'

Sally Mae was more than right about the men. One was an old prospector she'd saved from the deadly clutches of a whiskey bottle. The other was a young

Mormon lad, the eldest of thirteen children in a family that had settled in Sunset, up north near Winslow.

Havelock waited in Sally Mae's snug cabin, nursing a cup of steaming coffee strong enough to float hammer and tongs.

'Here they come!' The kid's voice cracked as he shouted the warning. Havelock heard him scurry to the mouth of the mine where he'd wait with a 12-gauge shotgun.

Now the sound of shod hoofs rang loud in the early evening as horses scrambled up the steep trail and onto the flat in front of Sally Mae's cabin.

'Sally Mae,' bellowed the burly leader. 'I sure hope you are ready to talk business about this here claim. You know I'm not a man to take 'no' too kindly.'

Havelock stepped from the front door of the cabin.

'Hello, Phil,' he said. 'Seems Sally Mae doesn't want to sell her claim. She's sent me out to talk business with you.'

'Howdy, Havelock. This here ain't none of your business. It's between me and her.'

'No, Phil. It's between *you* and *me*. Sally Mae saved my life, but you're welcome to try to take it, if you think you're man enough.' Havelock held his Winchester cradled in his arms, right hand on the action and the barrel pointed at the space between Jackson and the scrawny bucktoothed rider on his left. 'Just you and me, Phil.' Havelock spoke quietly, but his voice carried steel. 'Come on. How 'bout it?'

Big Phil Jackson knew Havelock, and he wasn't about to go one-on-one. The scrawny rider wasn't that smart.

'Come on, Phil,' he shouted. 'We can take him.'

The rider's hand snaked for his pistol as his spurs touched his horse. The horse was in mid-air when a bullet from Havelock's rifle smashed the scrawny man in the chest and tore him from the saddle. He fell broken and bleeding to the ground, dead when he hit. Havelock jacked a fresh shell into the Winchester.

'Now, is there anyone else who'd like to follow this gent to the happy hunting grounds?'

Big Phil glared and sputtered. But his hands stayed away from his guns. Eventually he managed to spit out:

'There'll be another time, Havelock. A time and a place I'll choose, not you.'

'I'll be ready,' Havelock said. 'You know where to find me.'

'Let's get outta here.' The thick-set leader reined his horse around.

Havelock's quiet voice stopped the mob once more.

'Phil. If I ever hear of you bothering Sally Mae again, I'll come looking for you. And when I find you, you'll wish you'da been caught by Apaches, cause they're a whole lot gentler than us Cherokees.

'One more thing. I hear rumor Buzz Donovan's been in these parts. I want him. I'll ride to hell to get him. He shot his own brother. You don't have to turn him over to me, Phil. Just don't be hiding him when I come looking, understand?'

Big Phil stared at Havelock for a long moment. Then nodded. He walked his horse down the grade with his toughs following meekly behind.

Sally Mae joined Havelock on the front porch.

'I don't think there'll be any more trouble from that bunch,' she said.

'Shouldn't be. But if there is, you just get word to me.' Havelock pointed to the sprawled body. 'Looks like his partners have left him behind. Wish he'd not gone for that gun. You might want to get your hired men to bury him.'

After the raider was buried, Havelock sat down to another cup of coffee. He figured it'd be days before he'd get another that good.

'So you're after Barnabas Donovan, are you?' Sally Mae asked.

'He stole the Vulture mine's gold and men are dead because of it. I've got to press Donovan so he'll either run scared or try to kill me.' Havelock's face tightened down. 'Either way, I figure to come out on top.'

'The least you can do is stay for a bite of supper,' Sally Mae said.

Havelock smiled, which softened his face and made him as close to handsome as he ever was. He didn't smile often. There wasn't a whole lot in his life to smile about.

'I'd take that kindly, Sally Mae. I've heard stories about your cooking. Probably lies.'

'Lies! Just you set yourself down at my table and see for yourself if you can come away calling them rightful comments from an appreciating public — 'lies',' Sally Mae said in mock fury.

Havelock held up his hands in surrender. 'I'm a believer, Sally Mae, a tried and true believer. All you have to do is get on into the kitchen and prove it.'

The meal lived up to every rumor. Swiss steaks stewed in their own juices, baked potatoes smothered in butter that

Sally Mae got from Verde Valley, fresh greens of what some folks called 'pig weed', lots of fresh sourdough bread, and tall glasses of buttermilk, kept cold in the depths of the Consolation mine.

★　★　★

Barnabus Donovan clutched a bottle and glass in a canvas-and-slab dive called Hank's Place. He poured a healthy four fingers in the glass and downed it in great, hungry gulps. His eyes took on a sly glint. This time Havelock would fall, no mistake. No half-breed marshal could outsmart an Irishman, and with $100,000 to spend, Donovan saw his way clear to become county supervisor, then go to the territorial legislature, and maybe even be governor. He was already mayor of Dead End, and folks in the White Mountains thought him quite astute.

Donovan got up and made his way through the miners to a card-game under way on the other side of the room. When the hand was finished, he said:

'Blake, a word with you?'

'Deal me outta this hand, boys. I'll be back shortly.' Blake left the card-game and followed Donovan out of the saloon.

The two men talked a couple of minutes outside Hank's, and Blake returned to the game in high spirits. Donovan crossed the street to a flophouse. He slept soundly, and left town the next morning, headed north. If Blake failed, he had another plan.

* * *

Havelock felt fresh and rested after a good night's sleep at Sally Mae's cabin. His feet had lost much of their tenderness. He could walk almost naturally now, except for the slight limp caused by a Yankee bullet in his knee.

'You see a big Irishman on a sorrel horse leave here lately?' Havelock asked the livery stable-boy.

'Yeah, I saw him.'

Havelock continued saddling his horse, waiting for the boy to continue. After a while, Havelock prompted: 'Happen to mention where he was going?'

The boy squinted at Havelock. 'He headed north out of town, but I heard him say something about Prescott.'

Havelock gave the boy a sharp look. Prescott. What if Donovan were after Carrie again, blaming her for Arch's defection or some such? Havelock flipped the boy a coin as he mounted the dun and clattered down the steep road toward Prescott.

Less than twenty-four hours later, he pushed the line-back past the hogtown at Fort Whipple and rounded the turn into Prescott just as the sun came up. He'd made good time in any man's language. Fast enough, he hoped, to pass Donovan and reach the territorial capital ahead of him.

No one fitting Donovan's description had stabled a horse at the livery lately, so the outlaw probably had not arrived. Havelock spread his blankets on the hay in the loft and went to sleep, leaving instructions to be wakened if Donovan rode in.

But Donovan didn't come.

Havelock ate his noon meal at the Nugget, then visited Prescott's saloons. No Donovan. He returned to the livery stable, saddled his dun and rode to scout the governor's mansion. Army patrols from Fort Whipple would not let him near the mansion, even when he showed his badge. Cassie had army protection.

Havelock put the dun back in the livery barn.

'Got any oats?' he asked.

The livery's owner brought a quart of oats in a nosebag.

The dun munched while Havelock rubbed him down with a gunny sack.

'Name me a good restaurant,' he said to the owner.

'If I had my druthers,' the man drawled, 'I'd pick the Bon Appetit. The cook's a Frenchy. He do make good grub.'

With white tablecloths and candles, the atmosphere was subdued and genteel, although some of the customers were dressed in rough clothes.

Havelock took a table near the rear of the room and sat with his back to the wall.

'Coq au vin,' he said to the waiter, 'and bring me a bottle of Chateauneuf du Pape to go with it.'

Pierre Martin, the French chef and owner, served Havelock personally.

'Monsieur, it is good to serve a man who appreciates good food and wine. We do not get many here who are aware of the niceties of gracious eating. You have perhaps visited Paris?'

'No. But I spent time in New Orleans. Liked the French food there.' Havelock forked a bit of coq au vin into his mouth.

'Ah. I see. *Bon appetit*, monsieur, and please visit us again.'

Havelock nodded, his mouth full.

The food was the best he'd tasted east of San Francisco and north of New Orleans. But he'd not yet tried the Bird Cage in Tombstone.

Night had fallen outside by the time Havelock finished his coffee. The wine he'd drunk didn't dampen his caution. After retrieving his guns at the door, he took a step forward through the door, followed immediately by a quick step to the right, which saved his life.

A rifle roared from an upstairs window across the street. The bullet made an angry gash in the frame of the door to Bon Appetit. Crouching, Havelock returned fire with three fast shots. At the third shot, a body tumbled from the window, bounced on the overhang covering the board-walk, and flopped to the street. Havelock rushed to the bushwhacker. He was still alive, barely.

'Havelock. Donovan's compliments. He's gone. Camp Verde. On over the rim. Hashknife outfit.' The man's lips showed bloody foam. He smiled. 'Said you'd be a sitting duck. Ha. You old wolf.' He dug in his pocket for something he gave to Havelock. 'For Donovan. I ain't gonna need . . . ' The man died. Havelock looked at his hand, which held a bar of Vulture gold.

'Anybody know who this is?' Havelock asked.

'I do,' said a man with a badge, who shouldered his way through the crowd. 'That's Nat Blake. Gambler and killer for hire. There's a five-hundred-dollar reward for him, dead or alive. Come on down to the office. I'll give you a voucher for it.'

Havelock stared at him.

'I'm Rodney Clayborne, marshal of Prescott.' Clayborne waited for Havelock to speak, but he merely motioned for the marshal to lead the way.

In the marshal's office, Havelock showed Clayborne his badge.

'I'm a deputy US marshal, but I'm usually town marshal of Vulture City. My name's Garet Havelock.'

Clayborne chuckled. 'Garet Havelock, eh? They tell stories about you, man. Some put you in the same corral as Longhair Jim Courtwright, Cullen Baker, and young Bill Bonney when it comes to using a gun. They say you're Cherokee. Staying long?'

'I'm Cherokee, and I don't reckon I'll be here long. Got a long ride coming up, I'll go get some rest.' With that, Havelock left Clayborne's office, voucher in hand. But he didn't rest. When the marshal thought Havelock was bedded down in the hay, he was well on his way to Camp Verde, the dun stretching out and loving the run.

Havelock beelined for Camp Verde's hogtown, a squalid sprawl of tents and shacks where an off-duty trooper could find anything in the way of entertainment, food, or drink. That same trooper could also find gamblers who were faster than the women, bartenders proficient in knockout drops, and whiskey just slightly more venomous than the bite of a diamondback rattler.

The trail had taken the new out of Havelock's clothes, so his appearance would cause no comment in hogtown. He reined the lineback up in front of the first busy saloon. Sharp, shifty eyes watched him dismount, noting he got off the wrong side of the horse. The same eyes followed him as he strode through the saloon doors. The owner of the eyes stood up and followed Havelock into the gloomy bowels of the hogtown bar.

Havelock sauntered to the far end of the bar where he stood with his right shoulder against the wall, his right foot up on the rail, his right hand not two inches from the butt of the Colt .44 shoved in his belt, and his Winchester leaning against the wall.

'Beer,' he said to the bartender. The beer came warm and half suds. He paid his nickel. With beer-mug in hand, he surveyed the bar's clientele. Donovan was not there. As he searched, Havelock noticed the sidelong scrutiny of a long lanky man with faded sandy hair, who had followed him in. The lanky man had also ordered a beer, and he held the mug in his left hand. His right was free, hovering above the worn walnut grips of an Army Colt.

Havelock smelled trouble. He didn't know why this man was gunning for him, so he acted.

The click of a hammer being eared back brought the lanky man's head snapping around to look down at the unwavering barrel of Havelock's Colt.

'I don't know why you're gunning for me, mister. But whatever the reason, it ain't worth it.' Havelock's unblinking black eyes punctuated his warning.

The sandy-haired man said nothing. He stood motionless, eyes on Havelock. Havelock could see he wanted to draw. He really did. But he knew now was not the right time or place.

'Pull your pistol out with your thumb and forefinger. That's right. Lay it on the bar. No! Turn the barrel the other way . . . with one finger.

'Bartender. Scoot that iron over

here.' Havelock said. He scooped up the pistol and turned to the sandy man. 'Now. Let's hear why you're gunning for me.'

'I know you.' The man spat the words out. 'You're Garet Havelock. No one else in the territory gets off his horse on the wrong side. You killed my best friend. You killed Willy Sydon.'

Havelock searched his memory. He could recall no Willy Sydon.

'Son, I don't remember killing any Willy Sydon. If I did, he was either running from the law or breaking it. There's no other way I'd shoot a man.'

'I never said shot. Willy Sydon swung from your hanging-tree.'

A sour taste came up in the back of Havelock's throat. He remembered Willy Sydon. A young drifter, Sydon had been unlucky enough to draw and kill a popular miner over a game of cards. A mob had hauled him out to the tree for hanging. Havelock, a new town marshal, had threatened the crowd . . . but couldn't shoot when the angry

215

men called his bluff. From the bottom of a pile of tough miners, he'd had to watch young Willy hang.

Havelock picked up the Army Colt and slid it back to the sandy-haired young man.

'You're right. I good as killed Willy Sydon. I tried, but I couldn't stop his lynching. A half-breed Cherokee like me just wasn't good enough. Now, Willy died because he killed a man he thought was cheating at cards. Turned out the man wasn't. I'm going to walk out of here. If you want to shoot me, you can. But it'll have to be in the back. Then you'll be in the same fix as Willy. Chances are you'd swing, even in hogtown.'

Havelock returned his pistol to his waistband, picked up his rifle, and strode out the front door. Sweat trickled down between his shoulder blades. He could almost feel the muzzle of that Colt lined up on his backbone.

Click.

As he reached the door, he heard the

hammer being thumbed back. Then the door swung shut behind him.

Havelock swung up on the dun. The sandy man was at the door of the saloon, his pistol still in his right hand, forgotten. For an instant, their eyes met, cold black ones holding faded blue. Then Havelock neck-reined the line-back toward Camp Verde. He wanted to check something out.

At the camp, Havelock stopped in front of a compact frame building that had 'Assay Office' written in bold white letters across the false front. Havelock went in.

The assay clerk came to the counter.

'Have you seen anything like this lately?' Havelock asked, unrolling the buckskin to show the bar of Vulture gold Nat Blake had given him.

'Why, yes. There was a big, tall gentleman from the Hashknife Outfit in here yesterday. Ollins. Yes, that was his name. Bartley Ollins. Said he'd got paid with those gold bars for a bunch of critters he and his boys drove to Vulture

City. He wanted currency, said it was easier to use. I gave him four thousand dollars for five bars.'

Havelock showed his badge. 'That gold was stolen from the Vulture Mine bullion room. I'd appreciate your holding those bars in your safe until I send you notice. I may need it as evidence. If so, you'll get your money back.'

'Why, certainly.' The clerk was taken aback, but promised.

'One more thing. I'd like a letter saying you have five bars of Vulture gold in your safe, and describe the man you got it from. I don't need his name.'

The clerk complied, his quill making tiny scratching sounds in the silence as Havelock waited.

11

The Hashknife Outfit — Aztec Land and Cattle Company — had driven into northern Arizona behind 60,000 head of cattle a year or so before. Already the name was widely known: partly because of the size of the operation, partly because its Texan cowboys swung wide loops. Headquarters were in Winslow, a railroad town on the banks of the Little Colorado River just north of the Mogollon Rim. But Havelock didn't think the huge ranch had anything to do with the 'cottonwoods in the afternoon' of Arch Donovan's message.

Havelock figured to go up Clear Creek and over the Rim. He'd hit Winslow first, but this time he'd not be looking in dives like the hogtown bar. With $4,000 in his pockets, Donovan would be riding high.

He planned to keep constant pressure on Donovan so he wouldn't have time to dig up the Vulture gold. And he rode out of Camp Verde at a lope, the letter from the clerk in his pocket and nothing in his belly. He didn't even take time to say hello to his friend Al Seiber, the cranky old head of scouts at the camp. He just rode.

Five miles out of Camp Verde, Havelock realized someone was on his trail. Anyone who wanted to stay alive checked their back trail, which Havelock did well. Rarely did a shadower know Havelock had found him out.

The dun horse was tired. He had spunk, but was without the spring in his big muscles that Havelock was used to. If it came to a mad run for cover, the dun might not make it.

Then Havelock saw an old trail. Just a faint breath of a pathway through the trees. Something most riders would never notice. He reined the dun onto it.

Fifty yards into the trees, he dismounted and went back to wipe out the traces of his passing. Should confuse the follower for a while.

The trail wound up, climbing wooded slopes away from the stream, an off-shoot of the Verde River, which Havelock had followed. Off to the right, he could see Baker Butte rising above the edge of the Mogollon Rim. Beyond that, he knew, lay Clints Well, the logical stop on the way to Winslow. Following that faint old trail wasn't a logical thing to do, but sometimes the illogical kept a man alive.

The slopes gave way to rock-strewn cliffs and canyons. Sometimes the trail was no more than an eyebrow across an expanse of red rock. The desert-bred dun took the trail in its stride, as if his daddy was a bighorn ram.

The sun passed overhead before the old trail topped out 500 feet above the stream. Far below, water sparkled in the sunlight, a ribbon of silver winding through a patch-work carpet of green. In the center of the clearing, a large pool reflected sunlight.

Havelock found himself on solid

rock. Here and there tufts of grass grew in soil-filled cracks in the surface. Otherwise, the sandstone was bare. The growth of brushy junipers and high-country manzanita started some way back from the rim of the cliff. Further on, gramma grass waved feathered stalks in the slight breeze.

The trail turned sharply as it topped out on the cliff, moving back away from the edge, a trail made by careful folk. Havelock walked the dun parallel to the trail, about ten yards further back from the cliff's drop-off.

Midway along, the trail dropped into a large crevice in the top of the cliff. Havelock backed the dun into a stand of juniper and tied him there. From a few feet away, the horse was invisible.

Havelock stripped his saddle gun from its boot and picked a handful of cartridges from the saddlebags before leaving the dun. He stuffed the shells in his pocket as he walked to the deep crevice. Far below, something white caught the sunlight. Havelock bellied down to the lip of the crevice, and saw a ledge about ten feet below. Small but adequate handholds and footholds ran down the red rock of the cliff, beginning at the ledge. The rotten remains of an ancient ladder lay crumbled on the ledge. Possibly, no one had come this way for centuries.

Havelock returned to the dun for his lariat. A jutting rock served as an anchor, and he lowered himself to the ledge. From there, he could make his way down the face of the crevice with those ancient hand- and footholds. The crevice ended at the top of a large cliff dwelling. The red rock of the cliff soared up and out to a lip at least 500 feet above the stream. The dwelling was four stories high, five in some places. Hundreds of people must have lived there.

The sheer size of the place awed Havelock. He found himself walking toward the edge of the dwelling, for the moment completely unaware of his surroundings.

The crack of a rifle reached him as he fell. If he hadn't gone through the roof, he'd have died. As it was, he found himself flat on his back inside a kiva about twelve feet square, looking up at the hole he'd come through.

Havelock picked up his Winchester, wiped it off, and started for the waist-high door of the kiva bathhouse. He catfooted, setting each foot down with care, testing it before putting his weight on it. No shots came. Perhaps the bushwhacker thought he was dead. He bellied up onto the roof, and wormed his way toward the edge. Once he could see, he waited. The sun moved. The shadows came. A flicker in the corner of his eye caught his attention. Then a horse and rider stepped into the sunny meadow below the cliff dwelling.

'Now, Havelock, if you'd just let go of that rifle, I'd appreciate it.'

Havelock started at the voice, for he had heard no one come up behind him.

'Stretch your hands as far out in

front of you as you can,' the voice ordered.

Havelock complied. A blindfold was tied over his eyes and a rag stuffed in his mouth. Rough hands turned him over and tied his hands in front of him with pigging strings. That meant they could be cattlemen. Or was there just one? Havelock had heard no more than one man. Still, he felt sure there were others.

Someone slipped a rope over his head and pulled it tight behind his ear.

'Just walk careful. Wouldn't want you to fall through the roof of Montezuma's Castle. Might be hard on the neck.'

Only one voice so far. Havelock waited for a chance. A spare second would be enough. But his captor was not the least bit careless.

Havelock walked hesitantly in the direction he was pointed until he ran into the stone wall of the great cavern.

'That's the end of the trail, Havelock. Even you can't walk through solid rock.'

The person guided him. Subconsciously he counted the steps. Fourteen to the left. He stood quietly, straining every sense to figure out what was going on. Then a rope was tied around him, going under his arms and around his chest — rawhide by its feel.

'If you fall on the way up,' the voice said, 'you'll have yourself to blame. We're using your lariat.'

We! There's more than one. Havelock had time only for a fleeting thought before the lariat tightened and began to haul him up the face of the crevice. Every tiny outcropping of rock, every scrap of rock-loving vegetation, every rough spot on the crevice dug into his body.

Although the journey up the cliff gave Havelock a beating, it also scraped the blindfold off enough for him to see with one eye, and he held the pigging string against the rough stone to wear it through. But when he came over the upper edge of the crevice, Havelock found himself staring down the barrel of an old Colt revolving shotgun with a kid on the business end. The boy didn't look a day over fourteen, but he held the scattergun like he'd been born with it in his hands. Black hair hung over the boy's black eyes, and Havelock wondered if he weren't a half-breed, too.

'Back.' The boy commanded the blue gelding, which was pulling Havelock over the edge. The horse did as it was told, and dragged Havelock a good ten feet past the edge of the crevice.

'Josie,' came a voice from the crack.

The boy didn't answer. He just untied the lariat from Havelock and dropped the end of it down the crevice.

The mountain of a man who heaved himself out of that crack in the cliff looked like he'd never took 'no' for an answer in his whole life. He towered over to Havelock, who stared up at him from one uncovered eye. With one hand, the man-mountain picked up Havelock effortlessly and put him on his feet, then removed the hangman's noose.

'Sorry to be a bit rough with you, Havelock, but I figured it was the only way a man could get you to come along peaceful.'

At a motion from the giant, the boy untied Havelock's hands and removed the rag from his mouth.

'Now just you wait a minute,' the huge man said. 'Lay off the gun. Let's powwow.'

Havelock gave the giant a slow, appraising look.

'All right,' he said. 'But let's get out of the open first.'

'Right here is fine. It ain't gonna take long. I'll talk, you listen.'

The boy with the shotgun moved off out of earshot.

'Ebson is my name,' the man said. 'Most people just call me Mountain.

'That there's my boy, Josiah. His ma was Arapaho, but she died of fever.'

'What do you want with me?'

Mountain drew a folded piece of paper from the bib of his overalls. Havelock had seen enough wanted dodgers to know that this was another. Mountain thrust it out, still folded. Havelock held the poster a moment before unfolding it and spreading it out. The paper smelled of wet ink.

WANTED FOR MURDER
GARET HAVELOCK
$4000 REWARD
DEAD OR ALIVE

Havelock handed the poster back without reading the small print. Donovan must have had it made up in Prescott. Wouldn't take long to set the type.

'It's a fake.'

'No. It's real enough. Signed by the mayor and all. Why it says right here that the mayor of Dead End, the town where you did that feller in, is a Right Honorable Barnabas Donovan, Esq. Description fits. Says you are an ex-US marshal and might still be carrying the badge.'

'I am. But I carry the badge because

I *am* a deputy US marshal. You can check with Marshal Meade, he's in Wickenburg.'

'Wickenburg's a long ways off.'

'You can cable from Camp Verde.'

Mountain thought it over.

'We'll ride to Camp Verde. You'll have to give me your weapons, though, and promise not to try to run off. I'd hate to have to kill you and then find out you were telling the truth.'

Havelock promised nothing, but he handed over the Colt. Mountain searched him and relieved him of his other weapons, but didn't find the bullets in Havelock's hat.

The three riders didn't get far toward Camp Verde before nightfall. Mountain Ebson picked the campsite carefully. The food he cooked was better than most. He also snored. The boy stood first watch.

About the time the boy was to wake Mountain for the second watch, Havelock felt a knife cut the bindings on his arms. He was free. But he didn't even twitch. <u>He</u> lay as if nothing had happened, as if unaware his bonds had been severed. He strained his ears, and heard a sigh of leaves against woven cloth. Whoever had cut him loose wore white man's clothes.

Moments later, the boy came into the firelight to wake Mountain Ebson. The huge man was instantly awake at the boy's touch. The giant sat on his blanket and shook out his boots, just in case something had crawled in.

Once dressed, the big man said something to the boy in a voice so low that Havelock heard only a murmur. He picked up the shotgun and moved without a sound into the darkness.

Josie came to peer at Havelock. Apparently satisfied the marshal was asleep, he went to his own soogans. Soon he was snoring, unusual for a youngster.

Havelock moved in fractions of inches, keeping his eyes on Josie's still form. The rhythm of the boy's light snores never faltered. Havelock had his moccasins on, as he'd not been allowed to take them off to sleep. Havelock worked himself to his knees and found his own knife sticking upright in a log not two feet away. The marshal grinned. When the shouting was over, that kid might amount to something.

The cuts and bruises Havelock had suffered when dragged up the face of the crevice protested at Havelock's movements, but didn't make him careless. He knew where Mountain Ebson would be sitting to keep watch. So he stood silently and catfooted noiselessly in the opposite direction.

A copse of trees stood fifteen steps away; the longest fifteen steps of Havelock's life. At the edge of the trees, he stepped in a badger hole that caved in softly. He went to one knee and froze. No movement in camp, and he could hear no movement from where Mountain kept watch. By sun-up, Havelock was fifteen miles away and still moving.

His limp was more pronounced now, and although he stepped carefully, he didn't try to hide his trail. Anyone who could sneak up on a man like Mountain Ebson did could probably follow a trail by its scent alone.

Then, through the clear Arizona dawn, Havelock heard the bell-notes of the Camp Verde bugler blowing reveille. Sound carries a far piece in the silence of dawn, but the camp couldn't be more than five miles away. He was almost out of danger.

Havelock lengthened his stride, his left knee protesting at each step. With luck, he'd noon with Al Seiber.

Havelock topped a rise and looked down on white tents lined up straight and fair. Old Glory flew from an aspen flagpole and figures in Army blue bustled about on Army-knows-what business. It sure was a pretty sight.

Barnabas Donovan. Mayor of Dead End. That's who had signed the wanted poster. No doubt he counted on bounty hunters like Mountain to get rid of Havelock for him.

A young sentry stopped Havelock with an imperative 'Halt!' Havelock showed his badge.

'Garet Havelock, Deputy US Marshal. Like to see Al Seiber.'

'Corporal of the Guard!' The young private went by the book. The corporal came at a trot. 'This man wants to talk to the Chief of Scouts. Says he's Garet Havelock, a US Marshal.'

Havelock waited in the increasing heat of the morning sun. He saw Seiber's big brindle mule coming down the line of tents. The scout had a game leg, too, and he didn't walk when he could ride. And he didn't let that leg keep him from being the best scout in the Army of the West.

'Howdy, Garet. Looks like you're down on your luck.'

'My outfit should be showing up any minute. I just need a little help taking it back,' Havelock said. 'You got an extra handgun?'

'Should be able to scare one up. Use a scattergun?'

Havelock grinned. 'Good idea.'

With a .44 Smith & Wesson Russian stuck in his belt and a double-barreled 12-gauge Remington shotgun over his arm, Havelock walked three-quarters of a mile to the hogtown bar where he'd drunk beer the day before. Havelock took a place in front, pulled his hat low over his eyes. and flipped the ends of the Mexican poncho Seiber had given him over the twin barrels of the scattergun to hide it.

Havelock waited in the hot sun. Sooner or later that mountain of a man had to ride in with the lineback dun on a lead rope, Havelock thought, but he didn't. Mountain Ebson came in alone, and he didn't come down the street.

'I reckon you're on the look-out for me.'

Havelock started at the sound of Mountain's quiet voice. The big man leaned casually against the corner of the building. He rolled a smoke with both hands, but Havelock knew if he tried anything Mountain would kill him. Havelock felt helpless, and didn't like the feeling at all.

The giant spoke again. 'Suppose you tell me what's going on. That boy of mine figures you're straight. If your story rings true to me, I'll give your outfit back. And I'll stand out of your way.'

'Let's do it over a beer, then.'

'You're on.'

Two tough men went through the door into the maw of the hogtown bar — one tall, painfully thin, and dark; one a giant, six foot eight and more in his bare feet and weighing around 300 pounds, all muscle.

'You know Barnabas Donovan, Mountain?' Havelock asked.

'Can't say as I do.'

'You make a living bringing in men with a price on their heads, but this time you're after the wrong one. Three days ago, Barnabas . . . Buzz Donovan shot his own brother in a gunfight at

Wickenburg. When I left to track Donovan down, folks didn't know if the boy would live. There're more dead people on Donovan's back trail, too. Two Mexicans, an old man who never hurt a soul in his life, the superintendent of the Vulture Mine's bullion room and his assistant, and at least a dozen Jicarilla Apaches.

'You know of me, Mountain. You've heard the stories. Yes, I've killed men. And I've let some go that needed killing. But surely you've heard that Garet Havelock does nothing if not by law or good common sense. My Cherokee grandpappy taught me that.'

Mountain nodded. 'I've heard the stories, Havelock. Though some don't cotton to your being half-Indian and all. Tell you what. You take your lineback and your stuff, and you go after Donovan. If it turns out that you're pulling my leg, I'll be after you. That you can count on.'

The huge man turned abruptly and went out ahead of Havelock, moving with the smooth natural gait of one born and raised in the woods. His shoulders nearly brushed the door on either side as he went through.

The lineback dun snorted his pleasure at seeing Havelock again. All his gear was there, including the food.

'I borrowed these from Al Seiber,' Havelock said, holding out the pistol and shotgun.

Mountain covered them with a huge hand. 'I'll see that they get back,' he said.

Havelock mounted and sat on the dun for a moment, looking down at the craggy face of the mountain man.

'I'd forget Winslow, was I you,' Mountain said. 'Like as not a feller like this Donovan feels a whole lot safer in his own town, Dead End. Most people ain't never heard of it, much less know its whereabouts. How 'bout you?'

'Haven't the slightest idea.'

'Not many do. It's a far piece. Up in the Blues out of Round Valley. Once you get to Springerville, you just get yourself pointed toward Blue Lake. Dead End is a skip and a holler up the canyon from there. But watch yourself. The canyon's blind. They say there's no way out except the way you got in.'

'I'll keep an eye peeled. Obliged.' Havelock reined his dun toward Pleasant Valley. He stopped over at the Tewksbury place for a chat with Ed Tewksbury. He hadn't seen Donovan. Further on up the valley, he bought supplies at Perkins' store. There he heard that Donovan had gone through two days before.

Outside the store, he cut the top off a can of peaches with his Bowie and forked the sweet fruit into his mouth with the point of the blade. His thoughts went to Laura. Taking care of her wounded brother, no doubt. Lots of woman, he thought, and turned his mind back to the duty at hand. Soon Donovan would have to make a move. *Cottonwoods in the afternoon*, he thought, whatever that meant. He drank the peachy syrup from the can and discarded it on the trash heap. The dun was ready to go.

Up and over the Mogollon Rim Havelock rode, passing Stott's ranch and heading toward Cottonwood Wash. From there, he went to Silver Creek, the place he'd chosen long ago as his future home.

The dun stood just below the crest of the ridge so Havelock was not skylined. The cabin stood silent just over the ridge. The man Havelock had proving up was not around, probably gone to Show Low for supplies. The stream meandered across a big meadow, green stretched out on either side. Havelock saw half a dozen new spreader dams to help make the most of the meager rainfall.

Off to the right the ridge flattened out into a bench, where Havelock planned to build his house. He thought of Laura and how she'd look in the home he imagined.

Plenty of room for corrals and the stream flowed clear and deep. Once in a while the sun would catch the silver flash of a trout rising for an insect.

Havelock sat there for a long time. He felt at home. A long way from the Nations, but home. It was hard to turn away, but duty called. He had given his word. He had a date to keep with the mayor of Dead End, Arizona.

12

Cottonwoods in the afternoon — that's what Arch had said to Laura. Havelock wrestled with the words as he rode. He gnawed and worried at them, trying to figure out what they meant. But they didn't make sense. There must be lots of cottonwood groves within sight of Eagle Eye mountain.

Here in the White Mountains at the foot of Old Baldy, the nights were cold. The temperature dropped with the setting sun. Havelock hunched his shoulders into the tough canvas coat he'd bought at Becker's store in Springerville and kept an eye out for a good place to camp.

Dead End in another day, he figured. Then he found the campsite he wanted.

An old spruce had fallen and now lay partly across a hollow. Beneath it, the bank was cut away by run-off. On the far side, the horse could be picketed away from casual eyes. An Apache on the hunt, of course, could find it, or a mountain lion.

A small fire, water from a nearby stream, a handful of coffee-grounds in the pot — this high country had a lot to recommend it. Havelock sat with his back against the cutaway bank, the fallen spruce above his head. He'd woven spruce boughs in the deadfall's limbs to form a rough canopy. The fire was warm and the coffee bracing. Still, Havelock took his Winchester saddle gun out for a last look around before going to sleep. As he left, he threw a few more sticks on the fire.

Havelock circled his campsite at some distance, and stopped often to listen to the night. The sounds he heard were supposed to be there: the shirr of an owl's wings and the short, dying cry of its rodent victim; the sound of the dun cropping grass; and the snap of a stick succumbing to the greediness of the campfire. Silent, yet not silent

— this high-country night.

Havelock went full circle, taking his time about doing the job and mulling Arch's message over and over in his mind. He picked his way back through a stand of aspen. Deep inside the grove, he stopped and listened again to the night while thinking about Donovan and the gold. Around him, aspen leaves rustled, a reassuring sound. He looked toward the camp-fire. He saw its flicker through the leaves as the foliage moved in the breath of a breeze. The flashes of camp-firelight looked like little round dots, which jogged his memory and he recalled another round spot of light he'd seen on the desert floor — the sun through the eye of the Eagle. Now he knew the meaning of Arch's message. Now he would bait a trap that Buzz Donovan could not resist.

That night Havelock slept soundly.

* * *

Havelock took most of the next day to find Dead End. The entire town consisted of six buildings. The saloon also served as a store. A large house stood back from the rest, up against the sheer wall of stone that cut through the green of the little valley. The mayor's house, surely. The blacksmith shop showed few signs of recent use, and three more nondescript dwellings probably housed townspeople. The single corral held some twenty head of horses, all excellent stock. Whoever lived in Dead End liked to be well mounted.

Havelock went straight to the saloon, where he planned to drop his bombshell; one that only Donovan would understand.

Three pairs of watchful wary eyes set in hard faces watched Havelock enter. All three men sat at the same table, a pack of greasy cards before them. Behind them, the stove crackled, cutting the cold of the highland valley.

Havelock bellied up to the bar. One of the trio shoved back his chair and came around behind the bar.

'We got whiskey,' he said. 'You can have one shot. Then git. Dead End ain't your kinda place.'

Havelock's left hand shot out, grabbing the bartender by a handful of shirt and apron front. A jerk of his powerful left shoulder brought the barkeep hard into the backside of the bar. Havelock's right hand held a cocked .44 Frontier Colt. Its barrel gouged at the soft underside of the man's chin.

'Just stay where you are,' Havelock growled, shooting a hard glance at the other two men. They froze half-standing. Then slowly settled back down in their chairs.

'Now, barkeep,' Havelock snarled, 'you ain't man enough to tell me when, or how fast, to get out of any town. And I don't want any of your rotgut whiskey. I came here to leave a message for your mayor, *Mister* Donovan.' Havelock screwed the barrel of the Colt a little deeper into the man's chin. 'Buzz Donovan *is* the mayor of this armpit of the earth, ain't he?'

The man nodded, his eyes wide and white. The rancid smell of fear filled the room.

'Then you tell him that half-breed Garet Havelock was here. Tell him that I'll meet him at the cottonwoods below Eagle Eye Mountain in the afternoon. He'll know what I mean. Got that?'

The man could barely nod.

'Be a good boy and give me the shotgun from behind the bar,' Havelock commanded. The wicked weapon was sawed off at both ends, 10-gauge, and polished to a high shine. Havelock released his left-handed hold on the barman and picked up the shotgun. Deftly he broke it open and checked the loads. He snapped the scattergun shut and shoved his pistol back in his waistband. The sawed-off cannon now covered everyone in the bar. Havelock backed slowly to the door. All he had to do now was get out of this robber's roost and back to Eagle Eye Mountain alive.

He went through the door and up on the lineback in one swift fluid motion. From the saddle, he gave the saloon door both barrels. The spreading buckshot nearly tore the swinging doors off their hinges, and certainly gave those inside second thoughts about following the man called Havelock.

The thunder of hoofs echoed the thunder of the shotgun. Riders rushed up the valley at a flat-out run. The group of galloping riders blocked the way into the valley, so Havelock rode off at an angle. He and the lineback climbed fast, and Havelock hoped he could find a way through or around the stone precipices that formed the dead end of the valley. Mountain Ebson's words rang in his ears: 'There's no way out 'ceptin' the way you came in.'

Shouts came from town. Toy-size figures milled around the front of the saloon. A man in black knelt where the dun's hoofprints started out of town. He raised his face toward the mountains towering above town, and seemed to look straight at Havelock.

That man's an Indian, Havelock decided. A renegade turned to the white man's ways of murder and pillage. In his mind, Havelock searched the wanted flyers in the drawer of his desk. Nothing matched the man in black. But Havelock knew that that man stood between him and the cottonwoods below Eagle Eye Mountain.

Havelock found the way over the top almost by accident. As he rode along the base of the cliff, an odd shadow caught the corner of his eye. He'd noticed nothing as he went by, but once past, he could see that one layer of rock overlapped another, and there was a narrow strip of level sand between the vertical walls, wide enough to lead the dun into, but not wide enough to ride into.

Rounded depressions showed in the soft sand on the crevice floor. Footprints. Large animals used this crack in the wall. It might be a way to the top.

Havelock had no choice but to get off the dun and lead him into the crack.

A hundred feet in, the passage started leading upward. The bottom was strewn with broken stone now. Man and horse stepped carefully. Twice Havelock stopped: once he went back to the mouth of the passage and swept the floor clean; once he reached back and hooked the stirrups on the saddle horn. Havelock forced the black-clad figure of the renegade into the far recesses of his mind. Still, he knew the Indian would find the passage, and Donovan's hooligans would again be on his trail.

Havelock and the dun scrambled the last few feet to the top over tumbled and broken boulders. The dun was mountain-born and desert-raised. He humped over the rubble as though it was just another trail.

Out on top, the land slanted toward Black River. Havelock drew a long breath and looked for something to close the passageway. Nothing. No boulder to roll into it. No tree to fell over it. The best he could do was get away, fast.

Havelock swung up on the dun and pointed its nose toward Fort Apache. From there he'd cut across Cibecue and Carrizo creeks, go straight over Black Mesa, and head for the Hassayampa.

Blue spruce, Ponderosa pine, and thick stands of aspen and jack-pine made the going tough. Havelock worked his way around the foot of Old Baldy until he hit a whisper of a trail that led northwest, made partly by mule deer and partly by moccasined feet.

Havelock chewed on jerked meat as he rode, and by daybreak he was in Fort Apache, where he rode straight to the sutler's store. He'd not stop again before the cottonwoods below Eagle Eye Mountain, so he needed supplies.

Inside, the store was dark as an old cave. It smelled of rank butter, aging cheese, and well-oiled leather. Havelock stepped to the counter.

'What can I do for you?' The storekeeper's tone was jovial and his age indeterminate. Wire tufts of white stuck to his bald pate just above the ears, and his small blue eyes held an amused twinkle.

'A side of bacon,' Havelock said. 'And cut it into half-pound chunks if you would. A tin of crackers, and one of hardtack. A pound of coffee, ground. Four cans of fruit. I'll eat one right now. Do you stock jerky? Good. I'll take a couple of pounds of that. Five pounds of flour and a package of baking powder.'

'That do it?'

'When you can get around to it, get me four boxes of .44–40 shells.'

The sutler's shaggy eyebrows shot up. 'Planning to start a war, are ye?'

'Nope. But I aim to be ready if anyone else gets the notion.'

Havelock took a can of peaches, opened it with his Bowie and gulped down the syrupy fruit. He'd sharpen the knife later.

'I'll be back in a few minutes,' he called over his shoulder as he went out the door. He mounted the dun and rode him to the livery stable. A good bait of grain could make a difference in the tough dun's staying power, even if it took extra time.

'Rub this horse down and give him a quart of good oats.' Havelock flipped a five-dollar gold piece to the young roustabout. 'See it's done right quick, OK? And put five quarts of oats in a gunny sack for me to take along. Rest the dun for half an hour, saddle him up, and bring him up to the hitching rail at the sutler's. Got that?'

'Yes, sir!'

Back in the dark store, and the sutler wanted to make conversation.

'Going far?' he asked.

Havelock grunted. He stood by the murky window, watching the road.

'Name's McFadden,' the oldster volunteered. 'Came into this country with Marion Clark and them. Clark, he never could settle down. Cory Cooley even beat him out of his share of that ranch they had . . . '

'How's the Apache situation?' Havelock asked.

'Well, Geronimo, Juh, and them took off from San Carlos earlier this year after that shootout down to Cibecue. They got three supply wagons about a month ago, but that was down in the Dragoons. They ain't been up here since General Crook got back.'

The provisions were in sacks, ready to go. Havelock tied their ends together so he could toss them over the bedroll tied behind his cantle.

The sound of running horses took him back to the window. At the sight of the riders, he pulled the pistol from his waistband. Donovan's riders were in town, the black-clad Indian in the lead, and the dun was still in the livery stable.

Green eyes in the Indian-dark face of that lead rider told Havelock the man in black was Juanito O'Rourke, outlaw son of an outlaw Irish father and his half-Yaqui, half-Mexican woman. There was no better tracker than Juanito. Indian-sharp, Yaqui-tough, Irish-clever — a hell of a combination.

Juanito had three companions, none of whom Havelock recognized, except for the type: men who lived by the gun and would probably die by the gun.

In town they slowed, riding by the store at a walk with eyes flicking in all directions. Only the dark interior and the fact that the dun was still at the livery stable kept the outlaws from spotting Havelock.

The four horsemen dismounted at the saloon and looped the reins of their horses over the hitching rail. As Donovan's men went through the batwing doors, the youngster from the livery stable led the dun toward the store. He came from the opposite direction and would not pass the saloon. Havelock could see no shadow of a man watching. Maybe they hadn't posted a look-out.

'Mister, your dun's outside,' the boy said.

'Thanks, son. You'd be smart to stay here with Mr McFadden until I get out of town. Those jaspers that just rode in are after me.'

Wide-eyed, the youngster nodded.

'McFadden,' Havelock said, 'I'm a deputy US marshal, name of Garet Havelock.' He showed the badge. 'I'm going to hooraw your town a little. I'd like for you to explain to the citizens after. Especially to General Crook.'

The old man raised a white eyebrow.

'You'd better pay me the four dollars and seventy-three cents you owe me for the grub and another two bucks for the cat'ridges,' he said.

Havelock dug sheepishly for the expense money he'd gotten from Marshal Meade back in Wickenburg.

'Sorry,' he said. 'I purely forgot.'

'Lawmen forgit more often than outlaws do,' the old man said. 'Can't understand why.'

'Guess we got a lot on our minds.' Havelock peered out the window. No sign of the four men. Maybe they were cutting trail dust with the saloon's rattlesnake whiskey.

'You two sit tight,' Havelock ordered. Outside, he threw the provisions across the saddle and mounted. Drawing his Colt, he rode toward the outlaws' horses. They turned to face him. Suddenly Havelock let rip with a wild Rebel yell. He spurred the dun into a run and fired his pistol into the door of the saloon, high enough for no one inside to be hit.

The horses bolted. One of Donovan's men came charging through the batwings. Havelock snapped a shot in his direction and saw him go down, clutching a leg. One man less, Havelock thought.

The horses fanned out across the flat, running with heads held high to keep from stepping on the trailing reins. Havelock kept after them until they were well past the old Indian ruins at Kinishba.

Havelock traveled due west into rough country. Gullies and canyons cropped up with increasing frequency, slowing his progress. He ticked off possible campsites in his head. Becker's Butte. Good cover. Big cave in the cliff. But no way to get the dun up there. Carrizo. Good water. Level land. But not enough cover, or too much. If a man had a good field of fire, there wasn't enough cover. If he kept to cover, he got no field of fire. Cross off Carrizo.

Havelock decided to water up at Carrizo, let the dun rest and eat some grain. Then they'd go out on the mesa and dry camp. He'd bed down in a good big clump of manzanita where nothing could get at him without making a hell of a racket.

The Carrizo ran clear and fast, winding its way from springs under the Mollogon Rim to meet the Salt River between cliffs of malpai towering 300 or 400 feet high. The best crossing was south of Flying V Mountain where the creek made a sweeping turn and a horse could pick its way down the south bank and onto a broad expanse of sand. Havelock walked the dun into the water while he was still on malpai rock, then rode him around the bend before reining the tired horse out on the north-east bank of the stream.

Far behind him came three men. One of them, a straight-backed figure in black, rode at full speed with his eyes glued to the ground. Havelock's trail wound. He never rode far in a straight line. Soon the trio must stop for the night. Even Juanito O'Rourke couldn't read sign in the dark.

The dun rolled in lieu of a rubdown, and fell to cropping at the thick grass. Bacon fried on a hatful of fire. Coffee frothed in the lard can at the fire's side, sending up an enticing aroma. When the bacon was done, Havelock added half a dozen hardtack biscuits that he'd broken up on a flat rock and a cupful of water. The water softened the hardtack and the bacon added flavor. The result was a good hot trail meal, backed by a half-gallon of black coffee strong enough to take the hair off a man's tongue.

As the sun set, Havelock bedded in a manzanita thicket. He picketed the dun in a stand of juniper close by. He was asleep almost before the stars came out.

13

Some thirty-five miles south of Have-lock, Donovan stepped down from a stagecoach in Globe.

'Ike Clanton,' Donovan said, offering a hand to the big man who met the stage. 'Good to see you again. Still up to your old tricks?'

Clanton shook the hand. 'Naw, I'm thinking about going to New Mexico, Mr Donovan. Pa's gone. Billy got his in Tombstone. You know, the Earps . . . Phin and me, we're figuring to homestead over west of Quemado. The way things look with the Hashknife and Twenty-Four outfits, we should do all right.'

Donovan's face clouded over at the mention of the OK Corral fight.

'Lawmen,' he growled. 'Seems a person just can't get rid of them. A marshal's been dogging me for weeks

261

now. He won't let well enough alone.'

'Who's that?' Clanton asked.

Donovan spat out his reply. 'That son-of-a-bitch Cherokee half-breed, Garet Havelock.'

Clanton looked up sharply. 'Havelock? You'd do good to stay outta his way. That man may be part Cherokee but he's all rawhide. Riders on the trail say steer clear a him.'

Donovan's face flushed. 'Juanito O'Rourke will take care of Havelock, for good. Come along. I could use a drink, and I'll buy you one, too.'

* * *

Havelock passed through the Tonto Basin and was nearly to Cave Creek by his second day out of Fort Apache. But no one showed on his back trail, and that made him uncomfortable.

Havelock mulled over the lack of pursuit. *I'll bet they don't even try to catch me,* he thought. Havelock decided Donovan's riders had gone straight to Eagle Eye Mountain and had already passed him. That night he dreamed of Laura, but when dawn came, he was already far down the trail, the canned fruit gone and one quart of grain left in the gunny sack for the lineback dun.

★   ★   ★

After a night in Globe, Donovan rode the stage to Phoenix, where he hired a light buckboard and a good team of horses. He drove into Wickenburg with a wooden barrel of water strapped to the buckboard and two canvas water-bags hanging from its sides. Desert lay ahead and behind, and he had a far piece to go.

Donovan counted on his fancy clothes and clean-shaven face to keep people in Wickenburg from connecting him with the ruffian who'd shot Arch. But Laura waited for Havelock and kept watch on the roads into Wicken-burg. She saw Donovan come into town and set about finding out what he was doing.

★ ★ ★

That night, Havelock came upon Donovan's men camped near the Hassayampa river. He spotted their fire and dismounted the dun a hundred yards away. The brace on his left leg groaned slightly, but his moccasined feet made no sound on the desert floor.

Two men hunkered down by the fire, staring into the coals and talking quietly. Havelock's lips formed a hard smile as he watched. Looking at the fire would make them momentarily night-blind when they raised their eyes.

The third man lay asleep in his blankets on the far side of the fire. That would be Juanito. Havelock catfooted closer. Neither man moved. They were lost in their musings, and now he could hear them.

'Ten thousand dollars!' said the larger man. 'Who is Havelock that the boss would put that price on him?'

'Guess he kind of cramps the boss. John Ringo was in Vulture City when a bunch o' miners strung up a kid for killing a guy over cards. Havelock tried to stop the mob, but they was too many and he wouldn't shoot 'em down. But I hear that was the last lynching in Vulture. After that, Havelock got downright mean. Just let the Cherokee in him come right out.'

'I'm still mean,' Havelock said, stepping into the light of the camp-fire. 'And I'm still Cherokee. Either of you boys wanna try me?'

The big one raised his hands high.

'Don't reckon I'm ready to die,' he said, throwing a meaningful look at the smaller man.

Havelock's instincts screamed. Where's Juanito? He'd not jumped from his blankets when Havelock spoke. And the two outlaws were too willing to co-operate. He snaked their guns from their holsters. One went into his waistband, the other he threw at the pile of blankets.

Nothing moved.

That's why they're unperturbed, Havelock thought. *They figure Juanito 'll pull their irons out of the fire.*

Havelock knew the half-breed was close by. 'O'Rourke,' he said. 'Listen. Commodore Perry Owens says you helped him out of a jam over to Navajo Springs. He cottons to you. Says you've got judgement.'

No sound came from the darkness beyond the fire.

'Look, Juanito. If you come in here, one of us will die, and the other will likely pack lead. You're not the kind to ambush a man. So why don't you let it ride? I've no quarrel with you and I don't think you've got one with me. There'll be another day, if you're looking for it. How 'bout it?'

Havelock listened. At first only silence, then the protest of leather as someone swung aboard a saddle, followed by the faint sound of a walking horse.

Donovan's riders were stunned.

'That no-good half-breed son of Satan. He's rode off an' left us.'

'He's a better man than the two of you together. Juanito O'Rourke ain't gonna get caught sitting by a fire with his britches down,' Havelock chided. 'I could take you in, I imagine there's a wanted dodger out on you. But right now, I don't think Arizona air agrees with you. You can go to Hole-in-the-Wall up Wyoming way, or try to bluff your way into Brown's Hole in Utah. Whichever, I don't want to see hide nor hair of you in Arizona. If I do, I'll shoot first and then ask what you're up to. That clear?'

'You can't send us out there without no guns. Geronimo's still loose and old Puma's warriors could be anywhere,' the big man said.

'You've got a choice. You can ride out on a horse. Or, you can stay right here, tied hand and foot, by the fire you like so much.'

The smaller man twitched. 'We'll ride.'

Havelock walked them to their horses. He shucked their saddle guns, but left ropes and canteens.

'I'm counting on not seeing you boys again,' he said.

'You won't,' the smaller one answered. They reined their horses north along the Hassayampa.

Back in camp, Havelock drank two cups of scalding coffee from the pot at the fire and used the remainder to drown the coals. A shame to waste a good coffee-pot, so he tied it behind his cantle.

Havelock made a dry camp, slept fitfully, and roused with the false dawn. Eagle Eye Mountain was blue with distance and touched with pink by the first rays of the morning sun. Its single eye glared at the desert.

In his mind's eye, Havelock tried to remember where cottonwood trees grew, and scribed the arc the spot from the Eagle's Eye would make on the desert floor. The most likely grove was along a dry creek that flowed into the

Hassayampa after a rain, some twenty-five miles away. Havelock hoped the oats would give the dun enough stamina.

The long-legged lineback settled down into a distance-eating single-foot, a pace he could keep up for hours. But at noon, Havelock was walking. The dun came along behind, head up and ears pricked. A hawk spread feathered fingers to the sky and screeched defiance. Off to the right, a gray pack-rat hopped toward home, a bit of glittering mica clasped tight in its paws.

Havelock stopped. He emptied half the water in the big canteen into his hat for the dun. The horse got two good swallows. Perhaps it would be enough.

Havelock felt uncomfortable. The hairs on the back of his neck crawled. He knew the feeling and could not ignore it. Someone was watching him. He'd kept a wary eye on the back trail, but there was no tell-tale dust in the desert except for a flurry near the stage road. It moved too fast for a freight wagon; probably a buckboard.

One swallow from the canteen and Havelock swung up on the dun. From atop the lineback, he could see the cottonwoods, their leaves dark green against the brown of the desert, still hours away.

The dun's step still had spring. He loved to travel and he showed what he was made of. The hair on the back of Havelock's neck continued to tell him that someone had eyes on him. He didn't like the feeling.

A dust spiral sprang up south and west of Wickenburg, moving on an intercepting course with Havelock's. Mentally he traced the intersecting point — the grove of cottonwoods.

Donovan.

Havelock urged the lineback to a faster pace.

The second sign of dust came by smell, not sight. Havelock pulled up the dun just to make sure. The taint in the air said someone had crossed the trail in front of Havelock.

The shadow of Eagle Eye Mountain swung around and lengthened out toward the desert. Soon the round eye of the eagle would pin-point where Arch had hid the gold. Havelock held the dun to a walk, keeping a sharp eye out for trouble, for trouble there would be, sooner or later.

The closer Havelock got to the cottonwoods, the more he had to detour around deep gullies slashed in the desert floor by rainstorm run-off from Eagle Eye Mountain. They slowed him further.

Havelock held the dun just under the top of the rise. Only his head could be seen from the other side. Eagle Eye Mountain made the head of an eagle with its shadow, including a flaming eye.

Now Havelock knew he could ride to the exact place where Vulture gold lay buried, for the eye of the eagle would light the spot like a beacon.

Havelock dismounted about a quarter of a mile from the cottonwoods. He tied the dun to a mesquite tree, pulled the Winchester saddle gun from its scabbard, checked its loads and the ones in his Colt, and catfooted toward the grove. A buckboard sat beneath the trees, two saddle horses tied to it and its team still in the traces. As he got closer, Havelock heard metal clang against stone and sand. He altered course to make a wide sweep around the sound. He still felt as if he were being watched.

He moved with Indian-like stealth from scrub to cactus to spindly mesquite to gully to boulder.

Two men dug in the dirt beneath a large flat stone they'd pried out of the way. Sunlight through the eye of the eagle threw their shadows long upon the ground. They piled sand and chunks of desert earth beside the growing pit. The diggers were the same pair Havelock had sent packing the night before. So the lure of gold was stronger than their fear of Havelock. He hunkered down to watch.

A shovel ground on something solid.

'Found it!'

'Come on, Bradley. Help me get this wonderful, shiny bull-yon outta this hole.'

The smaller man moved to lend a hand.

When they had six small boxes stacked up on the rim of the hole, Havelock stepped into the open, rifle leveled.

'Looks like you boys didn't take me serious. You should be out of the territory by now. Guess I'll just have to take you in after all.'

The two bewildered diggers looked at Havelock, blinked, then looked at the buckboard as though they were expecting someone to come to their aid. No one did.

'This will teach you gentlemen to listen to an officer of the law when he gives you advice. If you had harkened to him, I tell you, you would be much better off.' Donovan's voice came from the direction of Eagle Eye Mountain. A moment later he appeared, with a

Smith & Wesson Schofield in his hand.

'Get rid of the rifle, Havelock,' Donovan said.

Havelock tossed the Winchester aside. The loose tails of his shirt hid the Colt from Donovan's view.

Donovan turned to the two men who had dug the Vulture gold from its hiding place.

'Let me show you men why you should have listened to the marshal,' Donovan said, punctuating the sentence with two shots from the Smith & Wesson. A black hole in a star-splash of blood appeared over the left shirt pocket of each man. The shock kept each of them from making a sound as he died. They simply lay in the hole where they dropped, eyes open to the desert sky.

'Don't do it, señor.' The voice behind Havelock was soft, hardly more than a whisper, but it carried steel-hard warning. Havelock relaxed his right hand, which had been inching toward the butt of the pistol jammed in his waistband, and brought it back into plain sight. Havelock looked over his left shoulder. Juanito O'Rourke, dressed in black as always, stood about thirty feet away and slightly behind him. Donovan, who held the still-smoking Smith & Wesson, was on Havelock's left as well, twenty feet away and to the front. Havelock steeled his nerves, ready to take advantage of the slightest break.

Donovan eared back the hammer of his pistol.

'Havelock, you rode me from pillar to post. I hardly even had time to take a good bath. And a gentleman should not be odoriferous. Every time I thought I was rid of you, you turned up again. You've become very tiresome. I should have shot you through the heart back in the Indian Nations. I will now rectify that error, and make use of Vulture gold to obtain my rightful place. First county commissioner, then legislator, perhaps, and on to be appointed governor of this great territory.' Donovan threw his head back and laughed — the same laughter as Havelock had heard in the Nations, and in Vulture City.

Havelock saw death come creeping from Eagle Eye Mountain, cold and blue, as the sun went down. Deep down in his bowels anger caught fire. Under his breath, he started singing his Cherokee death song. If he had to die doing his job, so be it, but he didn't have to listen to Barnabas Donovan. Fury built behind his eyes, hot and red, without reason or logic. No one had the right to put Garet Havelock into a hard hole in the desert without his doing something about it. Pausing in his death song, he silently apologized to Laura.

Havelock started the death song again, and glanced at Juanito O'Rourke. The half-breed outlaw had lowered his gun. He watched Donovan with an amused half-smile on his dark face.

No way out. But Rothwell Havelock had always told his eldest son that there was no stopping a man in the right who just keeps on going. Havelock made his move.

Without a word, he snaked his Colt from his waistband, half-turned toward Juanito O'Rourke, and shot the outlaw through the surprised look on his face. The roar of Donovan's Smith & Wesson came an instant after Havelock's. Juanito's face dissolved into a mask of blood as Donovan's slug smashed into Havelock's torso, ripping and tearing and flinging him to the ground.

Havelock instinctively rolled. Donovan's second shot caught him in the fleshy part of his left calf. *Why does he always have to shoot me in the left leg?* Havelock wondered. He felt detached, almost as if his mind floated, separate, above his body. Every movement seemed an interminable crawl. He rolled over onto his belly, brought his right fist up with the elbow supporting it, and pointed his Colt at Donovan like an index finger, not taking precise aim. The gun spat flame, but Havelock was unaware he had pulled the trigger.

Donovan went to his knees, red wetness spreading across the white of his fine ruffled shirt.

'You worthless son of . . . ' He started to curse Havelock, but another bullet from the Colt tore away half Donovan's jaw and left the curse gurgling in a froth of blood.

Havelock peered through the darkness that clouded his eyes. Donovan toppled face down, twitched, and lay still.

Paralysis crept over Havelock's body. *I'm never going to get this gold back to Vulture City*, he thought. *I'll never see Laura* . . . all thought winked out.

Five men sprawled on the desert, and the dry land sucked at their blood.

14

When all sound and movement ceased, when the billowing gunsmoke drifted away, a shadow moved toward the still figures as Mountain Ebson materialized from among the cottonwoods. A glance told him the two men in the pit were dead. Donovan lay with his ruined face to the sky. Blood no longer flowed. He too was dead.

Juanito O'Rourke lay face down where he had fallen. Mountain nudged the outlaw with a foot, then held his rifle at the base of O'Rourke's skull as he felt for a pulse. There was none.

Havelock groaned and struggled to all fours. Blood dripped from his ripped side. A large pool had collected on the ground beneath him. He squinted, tried to focus, and tried to raise the heavy Colt. He couldn't find the strength.

Once more, he collapsed, blood pouring from the hole Donovan's bullet had torn in his side.

Mountain moved quickly. He kicked the Colt away from Havelock's hand, strode to the pit, used his Bowie to cut the shirts from the two dead men, and brought the cloth back to Havelock. He sliced Havelock's shirt to uncover the wound. The bullet had entered about two inches above the hipbone in front and plowed its way across and out Havelock's back. Mountain could glimpse Havelock's intestine through the hole.

'Boy,' he called.

'Yeah, Pa.' Josie was only a few yards away.

'You bring me that clean shirt from my saddlebags, quick.' Mountain took the shirt from the boy, folded it into a square several layers thick and slapped it directly on the wound.

'Hold this,' he said to the boy.

Josie held the rude compress on Havelock's wound while Mountain tore strips from the dead men's shirts to bind the compress in place.

'Pa,' Josie said, 'horse a comin'.'

'I hear it.'

When Laura rode into the clearing, she faced two long Winchesters. Her hand went to her mouth as she viewed the carnage.

'My name's Mountain Ebson,' the big man said. 'An' this is my boy Josiah. Miss, if it ain't too forward of us, who might you be?'

'Laura Donovan. Are they all dead. Is Garet dead?'

Mountain raised an eyebrow. 'Garet? And you with the name of Donovan?'

She nodded.

'No, the marshal's not dead. But he needs more help than I know how to give.'

Laura took charge. She sent Josie ahead to Vulture City for Doc Withers. She directed Mountain to lay Havelock in the buckboard on a bed of dead men's saddle blankets.

'I'll drive the buckboard toward

Vulture City,' she told Mountain. 'You bury the bodies and come after.'

Havelock moaned and tried to raise his head. Laura felt his forehead. Fever. She wet a cloth at the spigot of the water barrel, wiped his face, and left the damp cloth folded on his forehead. His eyes flickered open, bloodshot and staring. He tried to focus. His lips moved. Laura put her ear to his mouth.

'The gold,' he whispered. 'Gotta get the gold . . . back. Gotta . . . '

'Mr Ebson, one more thing, if you would. Please stack those boxes on the buckboard and lash them. Garet wants to take them to Vulture City.'

Mountain grinned. 'He don't know when to give up, do he.'

With the boxes of bullion secured to the buckboard, Laura could leave.

'Mr Ebson,' she said, 'you come as quickly as you can. We need you.'

'I'll catch up to you before dark, Miss Laura,' the man-mountain promised.

Laura didn't want to think of the sun going down. She just wanted to get

Havelock to Vulture City. She clucked to the team, turned the horses, and let them pick their way south-east. She'd driven hardly a mile when a huge black figure stepped into her path to halt the horses.

'I'm Tom Morgan,' he said. 'I'll drive, you look after Havelock. Puma's warriors will guard us to Vulture City.'

Morgan drove slow and easy, making the ride as comfortable as he could for Havelock, who muttered and tossed and sweated. Mountain's compress stanched most of the bleeding.

With the dawn, the party could see smoke from the cooking-fires of Vulture City. The old Jicarilla Apache chief appeared out of the brush, said a few words to Morgan, handed him a small bag, and disappeared back into the desert.

'Puma's taking his men back now,' Morgan said. 'He left some herbs his medicine woman says are good for open wounds.'

In her fatigue, Laura could do little

more than mumble her thanks.

Three riders met them as they approached Vulture City: Mountain Ebson, young Josie, and a swarthy man. Laura knew she'd never seen the swarthy man before, yet somehow he seemed familiar.

'With Tom and them with you, I figured I'd just ride on ahead,' Mountain said. 'Hope you don't mind.'

Laura gave him a faint smile.

'How is he?' the swarthy man asked.

'Hanging on,' she said. 'But he's got a fever.'

'Doc Withers is waiting. Let's get Garet to town.'

Minutes later, Doc Withers went to work.

* * *

The first thing Havelock saw when he regained consciousness was Laura standing by the window. He spoke, hardly more than a raspy whisper.

'Where am I? Heaven?'

At the sound of Havelock's voice, Laura whirled around. Concern etched deep lines between her eyebrows.

Havelock tried to grin. 'Where'd you pick me up?'

'Out on the desert east of Eagle Eye Mountain,' she said.

Havelock wrestled with the information and couldn't make sense of it.

'How'd you know where to look?' he asked.

'I didn't, exactly. I just saw Buzz drive through Wickenburg and knew you could not be far behind. He changed teams at the livery stable, and the man said he was going to hunt bighorn sheep. But I knew he was looking for the gold. You found him before I did. The shots helped, though. Mountain Ebson said he'd never seen anything like it.'

'Mountain?'

'He was there. He said he just topped the ridge when the shooting started.' Laura glared at him. 'Mountain said you drew on two men who already had pistols in their hands!'

Havelock tried to shrug, but he was bandaged too tightly for his shoulders to move much. Besides, moving hurt.

'I was just doing my job,' he said. 'Hardcases like them don't belong in this country.'

Laura scolded him. 'So you're going to rid Arizona of bad men all by yourself, are you?' Then her face grew grave. 'Mountain had your bleeding stopped by the time I got there. But you've still lost a lot of blood. Mountain laid you on Buzz's buckboard, and then Tom Morgan and I drove you to Vulture City.'

'Tom?'

'Tom. And an escort of Jicarilla Apaches. Chief Puma likes you.' Laura bent over and smoothed Havelock's hair out of his eyes.

'But why Vulture City?' he asked. 'Wickenburg was closer.'

'Doc Withers is here. Wickenburg has no doctor.'

Havelock lay silent for a while,

staring out the window. At last, he faced Laura again.

'What about the others?' he asked.

She found it didn't hurt her to say it.

'Dead. Mountain Ebson buried them under the cottonwoods.'

Havelock half-lifted a hand. His usually expressionless face said he'd rather not have killed her brother.

'Yes, he was my brother,' she said in a low voice. 'But he was also a thief and a murderer. He shot Arch, tried to kill him. And he shot you.'

'Arch's OK, then?'

'Arch's recovering, but he could be dead. And Buzz . . . I know, Garet, you only did your duty the best way you knew how. And Garet . . . ' Tears sprang to Laura's eyes. She turned from him for a moment to dab at them. She turned back to face him again. As she spoke, her voice broke. 'And Garet, it could have been you that Mountain buried out there in the desert. Then what would I do? What could I do?'

Havelock said nothing. He closed his

eyes so he wouldn't have to look at Laura's pain.

At last he changed the subject.

'What about the gold?'

'That gold. That gold! The only thing you could say out there was, 'Bring the gold'. It threatened to crush you all the way in, bouncing around in the back of that buck-board with you lying next to it, feverish and incoherent.'

Laura drew a deep breath. When she spoke again, she was calmer. 'The gold is in the Vulture bullion room. Except for six bars.'

'One's in my saddlebags. The others are at the assay office in Camp Verde. Donovan got four thousand dollars for them.'

A tap on the door broke into the conversation. Big Timothy Hunter walked in, limping slightly, but without a cane. The star rode well on his chest, and he had an air of authority. Behind Hunter came Doc Withers and a swarthy man Havelock had not seen for years — his brother, Johannes Havelock.

'Johnny,' Havelock's voice was still little more than a whisper.

The younger Havelock grasped his brother's hand.

'I was in Galveston when I heard you was havin' trouble,' he said. 'I came running, but you'd already taken care of things. As usual.'

'Thanks, kid,' Havelock said.

'Now you just move away from there, young man. I've got to see to the patient.' Doc Withers moved Johnny Havelock aside and folded down the bed covers. He checked the bandages that swathed Havelock's torso.

'You're a lucky man, Garet Havelock. Lucky, I tell you. Mountain Ebson said you turned to shoot at O'Rourke and that's what saved your life. Donovan's bullet ripped through some muscle and penetrated your abdominal sac, but didn't puncture your intestines. Don't think we'll have any problem with peritonitis. Somehow that wound didn't seem like something a .45 caliber pistol should make.'

'It felt like a cannonball,' Havelock said, grinning weakly. 'But that's why I prefer Colt revolvers.'

'What? Why?'

'Donovan had a Smith and Wesson Schofield. Pretty guns. Big caliber. But only twenty-nine grains of powder. My .44–40 Colt has forty grains. Makes a difference. Maybe that's it.'

'Good to see you in your right mind, Marshal,' Hunter said. 'Figuring stuff out like that. Well, Vulture City's been real quiet while you were gone. An' I made sure it stayed thataway. Guess you'll be back on your feet any day now. I'll clean out the office,' he said.

'Do you like lawing, Hunter?' Havelock had a good idea what the answer was.

Hunter grinned. 'I'll say one thing. It beats the hell out of . . . oh, 'scuse me, miss . . . ' Hunter's face turned red as he continued, 'er, it's a lot better than working a single jack twelve hours a day in the mine.'

'Just keep that badge then. I've got enough holes in me for one lifetime. I figure I'll mosey on up and over the Mogollon Rim. I've got me a little place on Silver Creek there. Think I'll finish proving up the homestead on it and raise good horses. And maybe boys. Johnny, what do you think?'

'Who? Me? I gotta get back to Texas. But I'll ride as far as Silver Creek with you,' Johnny Havelock said.

Laura said nothing.

'This man still needs rest,' Doc Withers said. 'Now you men get out of here and let the nurse do her job. Tom Morgan left some herbs for you to make into tea. You're supposed to drink one cup a day, he said. I don't know what's in those Indian medicines, but sometimes they work. Won't hurt to try.'

Grumbling good-naturedly, the visitors left. Doc Withers shut the door quietly as he followed them out.

Havelock watched Laura as she poured hot water into a teapot.

'I was thinking,' he said. 'I sure would be proud if you'd come in partners with me on that Silver Creek homestead. If you don't mind partnering with a half-breed Cherokee, that is.'

Laura tossed her hair and turned to look at him, her eyes sparkling.

'Of course, Garet Havelock. I don't mind, and I wouldn't have it any other way,' she said, handing him a mug. 'Now drink your tea.'

THE END

We do hope that you have enjoyed reading this large print book.

Did you know that all of our titles are available for purchase?

We publish a wide range of high quality large print books including:
Romances, Mysteries, Classics
General Fiction
Non Fiction and Westerns

Special interest titles available in large print are:
The Little Oxford Dictionary
Music Book, Song Book
Hymn Book, Service Book

Also available from us courtesy of Oxford University Press:
Young Readers' Dictionary
(large print edition)
Young Readers' Thesaurus
(large print edition)

For further information or a free brochure, please contact us at:
Ulverscroft Large Print Books Ltd.,
The Green, Bradgate Road, Anstey,
Leicester, LE7 7FU, England.
Tel: (00 44) **0116 236 4325**
Fax: (00 44) **0116 234 0205**

Other titles in the
Linford Western Library:

THE HIGH COUNTRY YANKEE

Elliot Conway

Joel Garretson quit his job as Chief of Scouts to travel to Texas and claim his piece of land. He needed to forget the killings he had seen — and done — fighting the Sioux and the Crow in Montana . . . But he soon has to confront Texas *pistoleros* and then, aided by a bunch of ex-Missouri brush boys, he faces the task of rescuing two women held by *comancheros* in their stronghold . . . In the territory of the Llana Estacado, New Mexico, the violent blood-letting will commence . . .

BLADE LAW

Jack Reason

A silver necklet was all that was left to identify the body of the man McKee found dead in the mountains. The brutal murder was the work of Juan Darringo and his bandits who had made the mountain ranges their lair of robbery and death . . . However, identification of the dead man was to lead McKee back to the mountains accompanied by a man intent on retribution. Now, forced to pit their wits against the cruel terrain, they also find themselves the prey in a hunt that will have only one outcome.

SLAUGHTER AT BLUEWATER LAKE

Bill Morrison

Drawing pictures of hard cases on Wanted notices was a tedious task for Nick Paget. But when he was asked to draw one that fitted his own description, he resolved to ride back into the storm of trouble he thought he had left behind . . . The shores of Bluewater Lake were lashed with deceit, lies and lust for gold. Nick faced drowning in a quagmire of evil. Sudden death was all around him . . . Now, in a savage gun battle, with the innocent dying alongside the guilty, he must face his enemies gun to gun.

MEREDITH'S TREASURE

Philip Harbottle

An amazing discovery in the mountains leads to some odd events in the Arizona town of Mountain Peak. A man is found dead on the mountain trail with no indication of how he died and no footprints in the dust beside his body. Mayor Randle Meredith is forced to provide some answers. Aided by his son Bart, his wife Jane and their Navajo servant, Randle is then faced with two more deaths. Now Randle's battle to protect his town from a murderer leaves him fighting desperately for his life.

THE GHOST OF IRON EYES

Rory Black

With the outlaw gangs believing that their enemy Iron Eyes is dead, the lawmen cannot stop the slaughter that follows. But one US marshal believes that the bounty hunter is alive . . . More dead than alive, Iron Eyes leaves his hiding-place to discover that the outlaws think he is no longer a threat . . . Loading his Navy Colts, Iron Eyes rides with venom to claim the bounty money for those wanted dead or alive. To him, that only means dead!